SORAJJEM

AKKINENI KUTUMBARAO is a well-known film maker, script writer and director of Telugu films, especially of what is referred to as 'parallel cinema'. Among the films he directed, '*Bhadram Koduko*' won the National Film Award for the Best Feature Film in Telugu in 1992. Along with this film, three other films, '*Patha Nagaramlo Pasivadu*,' '*Gulabeelu*' and '*Amulyam*' have won the Nandi Award from the state for the Best Children's Film. His film '*Thodu*', produced by the National Film Development Corporation of India (NFDC), won the Nandi awards in seven categories. Kutumbarao's contribution to literature through his writings in the genres of the novel and the short story is no less significant. Among his works are the novels, *Sorajjem* (1981), *Adhojagat Sahodari* (1982), *Venuganam* (1982), *Mohana Ragam* (1987), *Karmika Geetam* (1987), *Chedupata* (1990), *Amma* (1990), *Kolleti Jadalu* (2014), *Tholi Adugulu* (2015), and a collection of short stories, *Panivaditanam* (2005). *Sorajjem*, written in 1973 and published in 1981, won the first prize in the *Swathi* Novel Contest. Kutumbarao was presented the Sri Potti Sriramulu Telugu University Keerti Puraskaram in 2015 for his contribution to the genre of the novel.

ALLADI UMA and M. SRIDHAR have taught in the Department of English at the University of Hyderabad. They have translated many works of literature from Telugu into English, including *Untouchable Spring* (2011), *Pandita Parameswara Sastry's Will* (2010), *Bhoomi* (2008), *Water Song: A Long Poem* (2005), *Mohana!, Oh Mohana! and Other Poems* (2005), *Beware, the Cows are Coming!* (2001) and *Ayoni and Other Stories* (2001). They have occasionally translated from English to Telugu, significant among which is *Chichibaba Sodarulu* (2001; *Brothers from Chichibaba* by D. P. Sengupta), a children's story on nuclear warfare between neighbouring countries. Uma and Sridhar have won the Jyestha Literary Award, the Katha Commendation Prize and the Rentala Memorial Award for their contribution to the field of translation.

SORAJJEM

AKKINENI KUTUMBARAO

Translated from the original Telugu by

ALLADI UMA
M. SRIDHAR

Orient BlackSwan

SORAJJEM

ORIENT BLACKSWAN PRIVATE LIMITED

Registered Office
3-6-752 Himayatnagar, Hyderabad 500 029 (Telangana), India
e-mail: centraloffice@orientblackswan.com

Other Offices
Bengaluru, Bhopal, Chennai, Guwahati, Hyderabad,
Jaipur, Kolkata, Lucknow, Mumbai, New Delhi,
Noida, Patna, Vijayawada

Originally published in the Telugu as *Sorajjem* by Sweccha Prachuranalu, Secunderabad, 1981.

First published by Orient Blackswan Private Limited 2016

ISBN 978 81 250 6293 6

023144

31032016

Typeset by
Le Studio Graphique, Gurgaon 122 001
in Berthold Baskerville 10/13

Printed at
BB Press, Noida

Published by
Orient Blackswan Private Limited
1/24 Asaf Ali Road
New Delhi 110 002
e-mail: delhi@orientblackswan.com

CONTENTS

INTRODUCTION

'What is freedom?' retorted Sorajjem,
and would not stay for an answer.

Akkineni Kutumbarao (b. 1946) is often remembered as a film maker, script writer and director in Telugu, especially of what is referred to as 'parallel cinema.' Among the films he directed, '*Bhadram Koduko*' won the National Film Award for the Best Feature Film in Telugu and the state Nandi Award for the Best Children's Film. The film was about the problems of street children and child labour. Three of his other films, '*Patha Nagaramlo Pasivadu*', '*Gulabeelu*' and '*Amulyam*' have won awards for the Best Children's Film. Another film, '*Thodu*' was adjudged the Third Best Feature Film in Telugu. As a producer, he dubbed Attenborough's 'Gandhi' into Telugu. He also produced several tele-films and serials for the Doordarshan and private channels. Given this scenario, one seems to forget that Kutumbarao has contributed immensely to the field of literature through the genres of the novel and the short story. Among his works are his novels, *Sorajjem* (1981), *Adhojagat Sahodari* (1982), *Venuganam* (1982), *Mohana Ragam* (1987), *Karmika Geetam* (1987), *Chedupata* (1990), *Amma* (1990), *Kolleti Jadalu* (2014), *Tholi Adugulu* (2015), and the short-story collection, *Panivaditanam* (2005). *Sorajjem* was written as early as in 1973, many years before he shot into fame as a film maker.

Sorajjem is the story of a Dalit girl born in 1947, a midnight's child. For a male, non-Dalit writer, it must have been quite challenging to write his first novel on the discrimination of Dalits based on caste and gender. Though the Indian society is heavily caste-ridden, there has been a general tendency among Indian social novelists who use the realistic mode to depict the society as if caste distinctions did not exist. In those texts, caste exists primarily in the portrayals of characters who are professionals, like the priest, the barber, the cobbler, etc. Telugu novels are no exception to this. It is only after the Mandal Commission report in the 1980s and the subsequent Dalit-Bahujan movements that caste as a category has been put to serious debate in literary texts. The Dalit movement in particular has been responsible for bringing to the fore poetry, autobiographies and novels by Dalits themselves in all Indian languages. Prior to this, there have only been isolated instances of novels sensitively depicting the problem of caste. Kutumbarao's *Sorajjem* belongs to this category.

Written in 1973, the novel was published only in 1981. Though the debate between Ambedkar and other national leaders over the need for social reform taking precedence over political reform was fought (and lost) in the decades preceding Independence in 1947, it did not seriously enter the literary imaginary. Naming the Dalit woman protagonist of his novel, 'Sorajjem' (which means Independence), Kutumbarao historicises this debate. The novel links the deteriorating economic conditions of Dalits under feudal landlordism in villages with their being continuously discriminated on the grounds of caste, and Dalit women on the basis of gender and caste. Situating the novel in Choutapalli village in Krishna district of coastal Andhra region immediately after the freedom struggle, Kutumbarao creates upper-caste Kamma character, Brahmam, who represents Gandhian ideals. Through the various incidents that unfold in the lives of upper-caste landlords and Dalit coolies who work for them, the writer asks if the economic exploitation of Dalits would not constitute violence of a different kind. The novel also depicts historical incidents in other districts of coastal Andhra that followed the armed struggle for Telangana wherein Communists were brutally 'encountered' by the Malabar police for their active support to the cause. This aspect of the novel puts to serious debate the issue of 'state' violence. The novel also depicts the sprouting seeds of revolution in Dalit lives. As a Dalit and a woman, Sorrajjem experiences the worst consequences of the prevailing socio-political condition in villages and of male aggression. The novel also historicises the forced migration of Dalits like Sorajjem in search of livelihood.

Kutumbarao thus uses the realistic mode of narration with a difference, depicting as he does the lived experiences of the characters belonging to different castes and classes in all their complexity. As a person who must have experienced his early childhood during the years immediately succeeding the country's Independence, his novel may be said to have come out from his lived experience. There is no sense of nostalgia for the past, but a concerted attempt to the recreating of it. No wonder then that he is able to recreate the place and time in the narrative, where he is able to capture the intricacies in the lives of the people from different communities and economic backgrounds. It may not strictly be considered autobiographical, but it is an autobiography of the people, of the region. In so far as we come to know the life and times of the Dalits through the incidents in the lives of various characters, the novel could be viewed as an autobiography of the people. As it details the region and changing socio-economic conditions of the region, this novel could also be considered an autobiography of the region. Through the region, Kutumbarao narrates the nation. His is a sensitive portrayal of the lives of the underprivileged. The novel is written using the subtle variations of language – depending on the place, the class, the caste and the gender of the characters. Kutumbarao has a wry sense of humour and this is revealed in even the most horrifying of scenes in the novel.

We have not come across many novels depicting the socio-economic changes happening in the lives of the Dalits after Independence in any Indian language. That a novel like this depicts the real social and economic changes in the lives of Dalits should have been written by a non-Dalit years before such literature was produced by Dalits themselves makes this novel significant in Telugu literature. There have been two important Telugu novels prior to this on the lives of Dalits during the freedom movement by non-Dalits – Unnava Lakshminarayana's *Malapalli* (2008; trans. V. V. B. Rama Rao) and Mahidhara Ramamohanarao's *Kollayigattithenemi*, translated as *Swarajyam* (2012; trans. Vegunta Mohan Prasad, with a critical introduction by us). The Telugu originals were written in 1922 and 1965 respectively. Both the novels address the question of caste in relation to Dalits, but the precise changes taking place in the socio-economic conditions of Dalits in pre-Independence India have not been adequately discussed or debated by them. Kalyana Rao, a Dalit himself, addresses these questions adequately in *Antarani Vasantam* (2000), translated as *Untouchable Spring* (2010; translated by us).

The similarity in the names of Swarajyam, the name of the chief woman character in Mahidhara Ramamohanarao's *Kollayigattithenemi* and Sorajjem (a variation of Swarajyam) could not have been a mere coincidence. The location of the two novels is the coastal Andhra districts, though the events depicted are separated by over twenty-five years. Swarajyam, though not a Dalit woman, is a rebel in her own time, having been educated and marrying Ramanadham after her own estranged marriage. Even as we make the comparison, we are aware that while Swarajyam gains 'freedom' to a certain extent, Sorajjem is left wondering if 'freedom' will ever be hers. Given that the action of *Kollayigattithenemi* takes place in the early 1920s, this act must have indeed been revolutionary. The novel also discusses the issue of Gandhi's call for the entry of Dalits into temples. It goes a step further in Ramanadham allowing the Dalits to draw water from his well, an act of social engineering, to make them participate in the national movement. Ramamohanarao admits that his novel had been influenced by Marx's theory of dialectical materialism just as Unnava Lakshminarayana defends his novel, *Malapalli*, saying that it is not wrong to preach Communism or to encourage the union of Labour against Capital. True, both these novels in their own ways depict the clash between the feudal and the bourgeois ideologies, the conservative and the progressive outlooks. However, they seem to accept somewhat unquestioningly the Gandhian path of mediation between conflicting forces. Kutumbarao makes Brahmam, the Gandhian figure in the novel, the representative of a new class of leaders who will take over from the cruel landlords of the past. Afsar, the Telugu poet and critic, says:

> Brahmam who always invokes the name of Gandhi and propagates and puts to practice his non-violence, brings in "violence" in another form, i.e., in the form of robbing the poor of their livelihood. He brings the tractor into the village. … Brahmam's brain does something that surpasses this. Making the coolies believe he will increase their wages, bringing the coolies from the Nizam [state]. … There cannot be a better example than this to demonstrate what form economic "violence" takes in village life. (1993: 13; our translation)

Kutumbarao thus goes a step ahead of his non-Dalit predecessors by making Sorajjem, a Dalit woman, one of the central characters of the novel, and by making the clash between Capital and Labour, as represented in the conflicts between Kamma landlords and Dalit labourers, the central focus of the novel. By choosing the years immediately succeeding India's march to freedom and the writing of the Constitution as the time period of his novel, Kutumbarao raises the question of what these mean to the lives of the Dalits.

Applying the principles of constitutional morality enunciated by B. R. Ambedkar as elaborated in Kalpana Kannabiran's *Tools of Justice* to the study of Kutumbarao's novels, Telugu feminist writer and critic Volga says that *Sorajjem* realistically portrays how Dalits experience the denial of every right guaranteed by the Constitution years after it had been officially adopted. While the Dalit male coolies' demand for an increase in their wages ends in some of them being brutally killed, Dalit women like Sorajjem are not only denied their justified demands for a rise in pay as domestic servants, but are also subjected to sexual exploitation by the men in the upper-caste/class households. Volga says: 'That their not possessing the right to work leads to their having no food to eat and their being denied their right to life is writ large in every page of *Sorajjem*.' (1993: 46; our translation). She goes on to say:

> Sorajjem turns into an agricultural labourer when she realises that she would have to experience not just exploitation of labour, but sexual exploitation in the households of the Kamma landlords. There is no possibility of her access to food everyday. Even so she could not tolerate the fact of her being exploited not only of her labour but also of her body. But she knew soon enough that there had been several other women who could not but put up with such conditions. (ibid.: 49; our translation)

She argues that literature of the kind represented in novels like *Sorajjem* have the power to move people from societal morality to constitutional morality as envisaged by Ambedkar.

Elaborating the possible effect a novel such as this may have on contemporary readers, Gudipati, Telugu critic, says:

> The atrocity of quietly murdering four of the youth in response to their demand for increase in wages by half a rupee is unpardonable. It would seem that the attack on brahminism launched by Dalit writers and poets is far too minimal when we read about how Sorajjem who went to school eager to study is so terrified that she stops going there all together having been brutally beaten up by the Brahmin teachers. Why should the Dalits excuse upper-caste arrogance that says that they have no right to study for just having been born in the Mala caste? Dalits have every right to ask for compensation from the upper castes and the upper-caste rulers for oppressing them for centuries. What kind of culture is it that makes the government and the police machinery support the upper castes and treat Dalits in demeaning ways? What kind of civilisation is it that makes one look down upon human beings who labour hard day after day to give all kinds of comfort to others?
>
> Readers would experience such emotional turbulence as they read the novel. … Anyone with a cultured heart would vent their distaste and anger at those who have shown such caste arrogance in our recent past. There are enough incidents and narrative mode in the novel that provoke such emotional turbulence. (Gudipati 1993: 18; our translation).

One can imagine what the consequences of such righteous indignation would be when a Dalit and revolutionary writer like Kalyana Rao writes a novel. The significance of Kutumbarao's novel then lies precisely in the fact that it anticipates a novel like *Antarani Vasantam.* While Kutumbarao's novel focuses on how caste discrimination operates in a small village and its surrounding villages, Kalyana Rao's novel presents the saga of discrimination of generations of Dalits spread across several decades resulting in their taking recourse to armed struggle. It is the microscopic depiction of the socio-political and cultural dimensions of caste-ridden village life during the years immediately after Independence that makes Kutumbarao's novel a unique example of social novels in Telugu.

It is for this reason that we decided to translate and bring the novel to the English-reading public. Translating it was challenging as we had to bring out the subtle nuances of the caste-specific, region-specific language of the original. As has been our practice, we have given notes only at places where we felt they were absolutely necessary. At other places, we have retained the original words, for we were sure the context would tell it all. Suffixes like *gadu* (showing disrespect) and *garu* (honorific) are added to names depending either on the social status of the characters or their age. Depending on the way they are pronounced by people from different backgrounds, the spelling of the names of characters too change.

We have often been urged to state our theory or method of translation. Having been practitioners of the art of translation for more than two decades, we are convinced that there cannot be a one-size-fits-all approach in translation. The approach instead must be tailored to the individual needs of the text one is dealing with. A typical sentence in Kutumbarao's text such as this:

> Even as the piglet was screeching loudly in dismay as it jumped this way and that in the muddy holes, that little boy too was throwing the dirty water on his face and his entire body and stamping on the pig's faeces, while the rest of the boys were shouting and enjoying themselves, and were going round the huts, shouting loud and hard. (6–7)

The sentence is very descriptive, long and involved. There are many parts of the sentence that use the continuous tense. We could have easily broken the sentence into easily manageable short sentences which could have given better readability as sentences in English. But we have instead tried here, as well as in other places in the novel, to retain what could be loosely termed as aspects of the writer's 'style'. Not that the writer does not at all use 'simpler' sentences. We feel that the writer uses a combination of different kinds of sentences to suit the mood, tenor and tempo of the narrative. In the above instance, the description is not a still camera picture that is captured, but a moving, kaleidoscopic one. Obviously, this calls for the use of a different kind of sentence than what the normal English language would allow. Also, we have tried not to interpret the author (though we know that any act of translation is impossible without some kind of interpretation).

Or consider a very culture-specific idiom like this:

> 'What's there for you? You have a buffalo that gives two seers of milk. You have paddy fields. You have a majestic job. *You have things on the stove. You have things under the stove.* What is the similarity between you and us?' (87; emphasis added)

Of course the opulence of the upper-caste/class employer could have been suggested very differently from the way we have rendered it, almost literally translating the source idiom into English. It has therefore been our endeavour to capture the writer's style – the long and the short sentences, the sentence fragments, the idioms, etc. – for we believe these are an intrinsic part of it. The style is the writer.

In one of our unpublished papers titled 'Whose Style is It Anyway? Problems of Talking About Style in Translated Texts' we refer to Paul Roche, a translator of Sophocles into English. Writing his 'A Translator's Admissions' in his edited book, *Aeschylus: Prometheus Bound*, he says the following about his method of 're-creation':

> In my efforts I have been careful to watch Sophocles. Where he has repeated a word I have repeated it; where he is rich in assonance and alliteration, I try to be; where he is harsh and staccato, I try to catch it; where he has a ringing tone, I try to ring.* I have tried to walk and to run, to rise and to sit, with the Master, but never by imitation, only by analogy, transposition, re-creation. In translation there has to be a change of instruments, but the tune, the feelings as relayed through sound, must remain as quiet, as excited, as sublime, as intense, as in the original. (Roche 1958: *xvi*)
>
> *The reverse of this, of course, is not necessarily true: If I have repeated a word, it may not always be that Sophocles has repeated it.

We have gone on to say that

> [j]ust before the above quoted passage, Roche recommends "paralleling the force and beauty of the Greek without ever deserting the native genius of English" and "respecting similarities [between the languages] without at the same time attempting to camouflage differences" (ibid.). Read in the context of the close paralleling suggested in the first passage, the task

> of the translator seems well-nigh impossible, for how many translators do have this capacity? What Roche suggests is exploiting the resources at the level of language of the translated text. We wonder whether there are other levels, say of culture, of the identity of the translator, etc. that affect the style of the translated texts.

Revisiting this paper now, after almost a decade, we would like to argue that there is nothing unchanging and unalterable as the 'native genius of English' and that English spoken and written in different parts of the world now is continually changing it. Individual acts of translation contribute to this in no small measure.

In trying to come to grips with the text, Kutumbarao has been extremely helpful. We thank him for meeting us as often as we needed, and foremost for allowing us to translate the text. We thank Orient BlackSwan for once again reposing trust in us, and Antony Arul Valan for his meticulous and sensitive editorial interventions.

WORKS CITED

Afsar. 1993. '"*Sorajjem*", a Portrait of Early Days of Dependence after Independence'. In *Sorajjem*, Akkineni Kutumbarao, 10–15, first published in 1981. Hyderabad: Swechcha Prachuranalu.

Gudipati. 1993. 'A Brutal Evidence of a Certain Time Period'. In *Sorajjem*, Akkineni Kutumbarao, 16–20, first published in 1981. Hyderabad: Swechcha Prachuranalu.

Roche, Paul. 1958. 'Foreword'. *The Oedipus Plays of Sophocles.* Dublin: Mentor Books.

Volga. 2014. 'Sorajjem'. In *Santulita: Rajyanga Naitikata – Novels of Akkineni Kutumbarao*, 30–53. Hyderabad: Asmita.

SORAJJEM

– to Chalamgaru, with love

1947 AUGUST.

It must have been about four in the evening. But, it looked as if it was six or seven as the entire sky was enveloped by dark clouds.

Yenkadu was looking around to see if someone was there to help him carry the huge bundle of sticks he had gathered that day from near the seematumma trees at *moollanka**.

Yenkadu couldn't spot a human being anywhere. Thick vegetation all around.

Huge palm trees, seematumma trees, threatening to engulf the whole universe, tumma trees, peepul trees stretching out in all directions, gangaravi, banyan ... with all these the entire moollanka was dark even in broad daylight.

Grass that had grown wild, spreading across the whole ground. Growing under the shade all the time, the grass, that was wheatish in colour, had grown so high and fallen all around the place that it would entwine you even as you tried to put a step forward.

Tumma and seematumma thorns looked as if they were waiting to pierce anyone trying to tread on them.

This moollanka appeared like a small jungle. Here, big snakes would roam around with their hoods spread out.

It was in such a place and at that time of the evening that Yenkadu was hoping to find someone.

Soon some indistinct shouts were heard from a distance. As the person who made the sounds drew near, Yenkadu was able to make out that the voice was familiar. He knew that it was of Yenkatesigadu†.

---

* Literally, corner isle; a remote part of the village.

† Yenkatesu is referred to here as Yenkatesigadu.

To the call of 'Arey Yenka! Yenka!' from Yenkatesigadu, one could hear Yenkadu responding from within the moollanka – 'Ah … What's it! I am right here, here.'

Yenkatesigadu was frantically shouting – 'Arey, Yenka! Paddakka has pains! Looks as if she would have a tough delivery. Eeramma too is not in the village. They are saying she may have to be taken to the *avirikan aaspital*[*] in Gudivada.'

Yenkadu's heart was thumping.

'Come on, quick! Put the bundle on my head' – saying this, he slipped his hands under the bundle to take it on to his head.

'How would you carry it all the way in this tense situation? Keep it on my head and hurry … Wonder how Paddaka is …!'

Yenkadu started to run after placing the bundle on Yenkatesu's head.

'Wonder how Paddalu is! Clever one. If she delivers by the time I reach, I'd sacrifice a cock for Gontemma. Which hospital should I take her to? How will I? Moreover, the village looks worse than a graveyard. With the rains, it looks like a huge bog. Impossible to put a step ahead. It's so bad, how to take her? Even if we were able to take her there, don't we know how well they'll look after her! Better to be in the village. Come what may, at least the neighbours would help. If she is taken to the hospital, the doctors and the nurses there would treat her as badly as if she were a corpse and leave her in a helpless state … Leave that aside, where has this Eeramma disappeared at the nick of time?' Yenkadu thought as he walked hastily ahead.

Eeramma is from the Mangali[†] community. She had been a midwife in this village for over thirty years. She had to be present, not just for difficult deliveries, but also for normal ones. For the entire village, she was the nurse and the *compounder* too. And the doctor too! Finally, she was even the maker of medicines.

With the clouds dark and terrifying, the entire sky was ready to open up.

---

[*] American Hospital

[†] Mangali refers to the barber community; traditionally, Mangalis act as physicians and surgeons, treating the village people.

Yenkadu came out of the moollanka walking briskly and stepped into the eastern fields. He got on to the Koduru road, after crossing eight acres of Bhushayyagaru's fields, twelve acres of Devendragaru's, one-and-a-half acres of Sali* Parbrahmamgaru's, the temple lands, three acres of Veeravenkata Satyanarayanagaru's fields and two acres of Narsaiahgaru's.

Yenkadu was now running slowly along the road.

Narsaiah saw him and said, 'What's it, Yenkadu? Why are you running like that?'

'It's time for my wife's delivery. When I was clearing the hedge in the moollanka, Yenkatesigadu came to tell me that she had labour pains … Why are you going to the fields now?'

'When they said there was a good match for my younger daughter, I went in the morning to Mudinepalli. That's why …'

'It seems as if it's going to rain … I am off …'

'Umm … umm … go along … see how she's doing …'

Though he had spoken only for half a minute with Narsaiah, Yenkadu began running as if he had been delayed a lot.

By the time he reached the old mill, Yenkadu came upon Eeresam, Nallenkadu, Devudu, Yakobu and Nagesu carrying bundles of green grass from the thicket.

'What's this? All of you together?' said Yenkadu.

The five carrying the thick bundles of green grass brushed aside the green grass covering the eyes and lifted the towel tied round the head slightly even as they ran slowly.

'How come, Devuduga, all of you are going at the same time?' Yenkadu asked again, as he ran along.

'Nothing really, mamayya. The five of us have to cut and carry the bundles daily,' said Devudu.

'Our bosses are not just auctioning the grass but, by God, they're skinning us alive! All of us have to come together, cut and carry the grass. Because each of the bosses fear that one of us might carry more,' Nallenkadu added.

Yenkadu looked at the five bundles. All five looked like five mountains.

---

* Sali refers to the weaver community.

'If the bundles were smaller what the heck would happen to your bosses?'

This time Nagesu replied.

'Even when we carry such a load, our dora* mumbles: "How come you carry such a small bundle?" They may be auctioning at the same time, but they surely are taking our lives out, these mother– … Each one wants to have a bigger load but we don't know how to carry a heavier load.'

'You've said it well. My dora too is the same. "Is it just you or are the others too carrying such small loads?" he asks every time,' said Yakobu.

'What do you say to that?'

'Yesterday, I got really mad. "It's not enough just to say something. Put this bundle on your head and walk from the front yard to that water trough. If you do that, I'll bring back twice as much. If I don't, you can call me by any other name and I'll respond," I said.'

'What did he say?'

'What can he say? Smiling sweetly, he said, "What's this, you seem to be really angry," and went in. He knows I am not myself when I am wild with anger.'

Chatting, they reached Koduru bridge.

From there on, Nagesu and Yakobu took the canal route.

Yenkadu crossed the other three and thinking, 'Wonder how Paddalu is,' began to run again. He came on to the east lake bund and ran along the bund. At the Anjaneya temple some children of the doras were playing. He went past priest Pichaiah's house. He came close to Akkamma temple.

Akkamma temple meant the temple Akkammagaru built. Akkamma was a devotee. She collected donations and had a temple built for Shirdi Sai Baba. But no one called it the Sai Baba temple. That's because Akkammagaru looked upon collecting donations as a movement, led it all on her own for ten years, but died just as the temple's construction was being completed. That's why everyone called it Akkamma temple.

---

* Dora refers to the landlord. Dorasani is the wife of the landlord.

When Yenkadu crossed Akkamma temple and went near the banyan tree, Kodandaiah met him saying, 'Orey, Yenka. Saying you'll come bringing the wooden chips, you disappeared!'

'As I was coming … as there was no wood for the stove … I went to collect thorny brambles from the moollanka … In the meanwhile Yenkatesugadu came and told me my wife was not feeling well. That's why I am rushing there. If she's a little better, I'll come tomorrow.'

'Arey, since you said you'll come, I didn't tell anyone else. My elder daughter was creating a fuss just a little while ago that there were no wooden chips. You say you'll come but you don't turn up …'

'Ill come. I'll definitely come tomorrow,' said Yenkadu and started running again.

'Wooden chips! They want me to get wooden chips! Great lords who want to get everything done free of cost!' Thinking so, he crossed Krishnaraogaru's house and came close to the Mala* shore. There were two big lakes in that village. One was the east lake and the other the west lake. Both the lakes had Mala shores. The Malas could not take water from any other source other than these two lakes.

In between the two lakes, the village was spread from the north to the south. Towards the north, Malapalli was located a bit to the west. The school was on the bund of the west lake. On the other side of the school was the lake of the Chakalis.† They washed clothes there. Beyond that was a muddy lake called Bainakodu. That lake and the other lakes too were filled with lilies and lotuses which pleased the eye, and the children who went to bathe there enjoyed eating their fruits and flowers. Malapalli was located next to the Mala shores of the east and the west lakes, and adjacent to Bainakodu. Pigs would happily loiter around the bunds of Bainakodu. The pigs were solely responsible for all the 'buda buda' and 'guda guda' sounds in Bainakodu.

---

* Mala refers to one of the Dalit sub-castes. The locality where they, and the Madigas, another sub-caste of the Dalits reside, is referred to here as Malapalli.

† Chakali refers to the washermen community.

Yenkadu could only think of how Paddalu must be feeling. The thought coming up repeatedly and he stepping up speed …

After he went past some Mala huts, Mala Ramulori temple appeared in the middle of the road, as if giving him protection.

In the village there were three Rama temples. One was for the village doras and for the other upper castes. The second one became well-known as Salipeta Rama Temple. The Salipeta temple was not just for the Salis, but also for those others who neither belonged to the upper castes nor the lowest castes. The third one became famous as the Mala Ramulori temple.

Crossing the Mala Ramulori Temple, Yenkadu took off his head cloth, stuffed it in his mouth, ran as if someone was chasing him, and reached his hut in a few minutes.

By the time Yenkadu came near the hut, the pigs that were circumambulating the hut scattered and stood by the side. The environment was filled with the stench of pig faeces – a peculiar stench of filth – large, large flies, huge, huge mosquitoes swarming on tiny, tiny muddy potholes. That environment was as unclean as unclean could be.

Yenkadu who wanted to enter the hut, could not. Inside, there were women from the neighbouring huts. This hut which belonged to Yenkadu and Paddalu is not a *pushpaka vimanam**. Not even a bungalow resembling a pushpaka vimanam.

It was a hut where if five went in three had to come out.

Yenkadu stood outside and asked, 'How is she, Ramulattha?'

Ramulattha did not reply but Lachimattha spoke from inside.

'Have you come, alluda? She is okay.' Instead of the words, 'She's okay' only Paddalu's groans were heard.

Yenkadu turned his head. Looking at a boy running behind a piglet that had lifted its tail, five kids there were jumping with joy. Even as the piglet was screeching loudly in dismay as it jumped this way and that in the muddy holes, that little boy too was throwing the dirty water on his face and his entire body and stamping on the

* Mythological aircraft which is said to have the ability to expand to accommodate any number of passengers.

pig's faeces, while the rest of the boys were shouting and enjoying themselves, and were going round the huts, shouting loud and hard.

In the meanwhile, Yenkadu heard Satyanarayanagaru scream from the front of Iswarudu's hut, a few huts away from his own.

Yenkadu peeped in and asked, 'Lachimattha, do you need anything?'

'How innocently he is talking! What was needed or not you have already done, haven't you, alluda? You are now talking as if you care a lot. Asking if I need anything ...' Lachimattha went on. The women inside laughed so hard that Yenkadu could not hear Paddalu's groans.

Yenkadu who was standing outside was very upset. 'When Paddalu is suffering so much how come they are having fun? Is this a time for laughing?' Thinking in this manner, he stood there for a while.

It was not possible to go in. How long was he to stand outside? Satyanarayanagaru's screams became frequent.

'What is his problem? They said Iswarudu was down with fever and lying in bed.' Thinking so, he went that way.

Iswarudu's wife, Sayitri was standing outside and trying to placate Satyanarayana. Satyanarayanagaru was unimpressed.

'What's it, dora?' Yenkadu asked.

'What do you mean by that, Yenka? This Iswarudu is taking my life out! Three days ago I went to Meduru. When I came back today, I found the cattle shed not quite like a cattle shed. There was not a drop of water at home. When the cows and the bulls saw me they cried hoarse, "Amba, amba". There was not a bit of hay for them to eat. The house was not quite like a house. It was like a graveyard. When I asked her what's all this?, she said, "Iswarudu didn't come. What could I do?" As for my elder son, he's living in Gudivada saying he won't come back till after his exams. The younger one has cough and cold. And now, when I have come to this fellow, he covers himself up with a blanket on seeing me.'

'He's been suffering from high fever since you left. Even so, did he listen when we asked him not to go? He said "Dora too isn't in the village, how can I not go?" and went yesterday and the day before too. Even today he set out to go, but felt giddy and collapsed on his way, in the bazaar. Place your hand on his body and feel, dora. It is burning hot. He is very critical. Has he ever absented himself except when he is very sick?' Sayitri said.

'It's not *his* life or death but my death. In fact, I kept telling him like one tells a parrot – "I am going now. Take care of the house, the cattle." How could I think that once I leave, he would hoodwink me like this? Even so, you bastards … I always knew I shouldn't trust any of you …'

'Wait, dora. Let me go in and see,' Yenkadu went in and placed his hand on Iswarudu's body. Iswarudu opened his eyes, turned slowly towards Yenkadu, and tried to say something, but couldn't manage even a word. His body was scalding hot.

Yenkadu thought to himself, 'Wonder if this fellow will live! His face has the look of death.' Yenkadu came out and said, 'Dora, he is really very sick. If you touch his body, you'll know, it's scalding hot. He is unable to utter even a word. Osey Sayitri, why don't you send word to your brother? Maybe he can come and take him at least to Gudivada.'

'That's what I'm thinking, bavayya. The children won't go. How can I leave him alone like this and go to Dentukuru?' Sayitri was in tears.

'Chi, you mother– … wretched bastards … all of you,' Satyanarayanagaru turned to walk away in disgust.

'No. It's true, I actually felt him,' said Yenkadu.

'All of you are together, aren't you?' Satyanarayanagaru said, and left.

'Doras are just like this. Even a corpse has to go and work,' Thinking so Yenkadu said, 'Your akka is having labour pains. Otherwise, I would have gone and called your brother myself.'

'Don't worry bavayya. Martamma left our place just now and said she'd send her son. I will put up with my woes. Go and find out how akka is,' she replied.

Yenkadu turned towards his hut. Paddalu's groans were louder than before.

Eeramma, the midwife, appeared at a distance. He felt as if a goddess who would grant boons had appeared before him.

He ran shouting out to her, 'Eerammagoru, Eerammagoru.' Eeramma was stone-deaf. She kept walking swiftly, shaking her head. Yenkadu who kept shouting, overtook Eeramma, stood in front of her and told her about his wife's condition.

Eeramma turned back immediately. She walked briskly and entered the hut in which Paddalu lay. As soon as she entered, she surveyed the entire hut. The string cot on which Paddalu lay had sagged. She named and abused all those who were present there. She then made them spread out pieces of mat and old clothes on the floor, and made Paddalu lie down on it, shouting, 'Not one whore knows ... but each one delivers a dozen. If she lies down in this cramped space, this whore won't deliver even in ten years.'

Eeramma did not consider herself deaf. She thought the whole world was deaf. So she would shout whenever she needed to say something.

The rain started pouring heavily. In a little while, it began raining even inside the hut.

Yenkatesigadu, dripping with water, brought the brambles, went to the rear of the hut, threw them there and came to the front.

People inside the hut were getting wet just as those outside.

In the rain, in that cold, Paddalu, with a loud scream, delivered a baby girl. Eeramma gently slapped the child as she was not crying. She held her by the legs and turned her around. She held her upside down. The girl started to weep loudly.

The sun was rising in the east.

The rain had let up.

IN THE MORNING the entire village was muddy and chaotic.

A *mike* had entered the village, with the songs, '*Swatantrame maajanmahakkani chatandi* ...' ('Proclaim independence is our birthright ...')*, '*Vande Mataram, Vande Mataram*' and tri-coloured flags, the whole village was agog with excitement.

Brahmamgaru set out from a bungalow in the centre of the village, followed by some elders, gave a darshan in Malapalli,

* A popular patriotic song sung by Ghantasala Venkateswara Rao.

sanctified it and asked the people there, 'What does independence mean?'

The Malas there were embarrassed to reply to him what independence meant. Brahmamgaru turned to another side. A young man called Narayana Rao was present there. He looked at Brahmamgaru and gave a sweet smile.

'You, Narayana Rao, you are an educated person. At least you can say – what does independence mean?'

Narayana Rao cleared his throat and said, 'Independence means complete independence. The white man's rule has ended. It's now our rule. We look after our needs and well-being. We have become independent now.'

Brahmamgaru was very happy. For having understood the meaning of independence, he said, 'Well said! That's what it means … But did the white man's rule end on its own? No, all of us together put an end to it. Gandhigaru … our Pandit Nehrugaru … our Patelgaru … our Prakasam Pantulugaru … not just one, but many great people … they led us from the front, fought against the whites, waged a war, a war without swords, with non-violence and fasts … creating fear in the whites with such invisible weapons, we retrieved our nation. They plundered. The white man took away all our riches to his own land. That's why he laid these railway lines. That's why we went to Moturu and pulled out the railway tracks … As for our leaders … they are great people. We did whatever they asked us to do … With that blow, the white man pulled out his flag and left saying, "Okay, people. We are giving your country back to you. Do what you like with it." We all went to our Angaluru and saw Mahatma Gandhi. You know all that. He is not a man. A God! It means he was born among us to wipe away our troubles and save us … That's why we have become independent. We must live together as brothers. If the older brother scolds or gives a slap, will the younger one protest? No, he won't. Just like that, we must live together in unity and share our happiness and misery … Now look at grass – a blade of grass. He tears it to shreds. Look, even that tiny tot with a runny nose.' When he pointed to a tiny tot running through the legs of the older people, the entire crowd turned to look at him and started laughing.

On hearing them laugh, Brahmamgaru was inspired. 'Our Yenkadu will tie a rope around ten or twelve such blades. If we tie that bundle to an elephant ... even the elephant cannot break it. That's what unity means ... Unity is strength, our elders said. That's how we drove away the whites. That's why our nation came back to us. The whites are foreigners. They made our nation too foreign. Now we have retrieved our nation. That's why our country is independent now. Our Yenkadu's daughter was born at this happy moment ... at night, like our freedom ... that's why I am naming her "Sorajjem".' As soon as he said this, everyone said, 'Jai *Sorajjem.*' When Brahmamgaru said, 'Hail Independent India,' everyone said, 'Jai.'

'Mahatma Gandhi ...'

'Jai!'

'Jawaharlal Nehru ...'

'Jai!'

Narayana Rao added, 'Brahmamgaru ...' and the entire crowd replied, 'Jai!'

Brahmamgaru distributed sugar candy to all the children present there. The children rushed for the candy and fell down.

All the children born on that day have these names – Swarajyam, Swarajyalakshmi, Gandhi, Nehru, Bapuji. Rather than keep these names as such, they added their caste tags to them. Bapuji Choudhary*, Subhash Chandrareddy. Some went a little further – Andhrareddy, Bharatkumar ... like these.

The mike was still on in Malapalli after the meeting. They had tied flags.The weather was cool, although it hadn't rained. In the hut, Sorajjem was sleeping. As the wet bramble sticks could not be lit with a match stick, even after her eyes had watered due to the smoke, Paddalu kept blowing the stove. Her eyes were burning. Her stomach too was burning with hunger.

Yenkadu was sitting on his haunches on a stone and thinking.

'Independence – why does Bemmamgaru keep saying independence? The other day, we pulled out the fish plates of the railway track near Moturu. Then too we shouted "Vande Mataram"

* Choudhary and Reddy are upper-caste names.

just like now. We shouted that the white man's rule must go. But did the white man's rule end with just that? They say he is a very intelligent person. Did such an intelligent brain desert him? If it were just to remove the fish plates and scream we would have done it long ago, wouldn't we? Why did we keep quiet for so many years … ah … there were no trains then. Maybe that's why we couldn't get independence. The white man on the whole seems to be an idiot. If he had not laid the railway lines, he needn't have given independence to our country. That is to say he poked his eyes with his own finger!

'But why does Bemmamgaru say, "We are all equal. We are brothers"? As for him he's a Kamma dora. As for us we are Malas. Gandhigoru says don't call yourselves "Malas". Call yourselves "Harijans". How can we be brothers? Can't understand any of this …'

As Yenkadu was thinking, he remembered an incident that had happened a month ago in the marshy fields. When Ravulugadu revolted against Pesadubabu, Bemmamgaru came and caught hold of Ravudu and said, "Calm down, calm down." Pesadubabu took that as a cue and slapped Ravulugadu left and right on his cheeks. When Ravulugadu got incensed and tried to get out of Bemmamgaru's hold, the Kamma doras said, "How dare you confront Bemmamgaru?" This man who said we were all brothers could have taken Pesadubabu aside, why didn't he do that?

'Even when the fish plates were removed … it was the same thing. We were put in jail. Everyone. Bemmamgaru had everyone work hard for him. He chatted with the officials in the jail and got *garelu* to eat from outside. He would hide them and eat. Everyone's mouth would water.

'"Rascals! How dare you look like that?" he would say, looking at us as if we were insects, but would not even throw a piece at us. But today, he says we are all brothers. Will brothers behave like this?' Yenkadu thought.

'Bemmamgaru is saying we are all brothers, isn't he? Do you think everyone will become like that?' asked Paddalu.

'Osey, you stupid one, just because they say we are all one, will Kamma doras become Malas? Will Malas become Kamma doras?'

'Why is he saying so then?'

'He will say it. Don't you go and sit next to him in the future thinking we are brothers!'

'As if … I only thought they would give us some land.'

'Aa … they will give us! That Bemmamgaru is your brother, right? Okay, he'll take out a bit from his wetland and give it to you.'

'As if he's that just for me! He's your brother too. He said we were *all* brothers.'

'What's it for them, they are great lords! They'll say all kinds of things. They'll do anything.'

'So, even if the white man has gone, our lives are just the same then.'

'What else?'

'I don't know! I believe Gandhigoru and others saying that they would see to it that the lives of Harijans will improve.'

'I don't know. Let's wait and see.'

'If only we get a small piece of land …'

'Aa … we'll get it …' Yenkadu was lost in thought again.

In his thoughts … Bemmamgaru sitting on a cot … two or three Malas standing far away with folded hands in the verandah … when one of them is thirsty, Bemmamgaru shouting and warning him to be at a distance, pouring water from a height from a pot into his cupped hands … Would all this disappear, would everyone live together? Rather than asking them to eat last, after everyone else has eaten in weddings and feasts … would everyone sit together and eat? Will Kammas allow Malas to enter the Rama temple? Will Kamma doras marry Mala girls? Will Kamma doras give their girls in marriage to Malas? Would all this ever happen?

SALIPETA WAS FULL of Salis. Chakalipeta was full of Chakalis. Kamma doras were in a *peta** that had no name. Malapalli was full of Malas and Madigas … just as it was, generation after generation. Choutapalli was just like that even now.

* *Peta* is a locality in a village or town.

At a short distance from the west lake was the Chakali lake. Fields surrounded it. The village's big school … between the Chakali lake and the west lake. It had classes up to the eighth.

The Chakalis would go to work at the Chakali lake and the children would go to study at the school at the same time.

Even as the children recited, '*Thallee, ninnu dalanchi pustakam chetanboonitin*' ('Mother, I have held the book in my hand thinking of you')*…

The Chakalis would pick up the clothes and beat them on a rock without thinking of anyone. With the enthusiasm those words gave them, they made several sounds like, '*issha*,' '*yeyye*' and '*ahva*' for every beat to forget the physical toil. As all the windows opened towards the Chakali lake, the sound of the Chakalis would resound in the school, and fill the Chakalis there and the children here with enthusiasm and exuberance.

Sitting morose on wooden chairs, the teachers would keep thinking of a match for a daughter who was above twenty, or about a son who did not write except to ask them to send a money order, or about their retirement two years hence, or about the farm they had started cultivating hoping to save a few rupees, or about the report the school inspector who had visited the school just a few days ago would write about them.

Sorajjem had just about begun to recognise that din, that chaos, of children coming and going, the elephant-like tread of the teachers. If one came to the Mala bank of the western lake, everything was visible.

Sorrajjem's father, Yenkadu would go for the coolie work he would get now and then. Her mother would go to the fields and follow the cattle in hope. She would collect dung, make cakes and sell them. Yenkadu would not get much work. So he would memorise the poems hard for the Krishna's role in plays to be staged at the Mala Ramulori temple.

---

* Song sung for goddess Saraswati, recited as the school prayer.

If Yenkadu found Sorajjem crying he would break into a song … '*Cheliyo Chellako*'* – along with abhinaya and emote it in the tune '*aa … aaaaaa …*' just like Abburi†. At first, out of fear of this tune, and later having got used to it, Sorajjem would stop crying.

Sorajjem had a brother, Tirapatigadu. Robust, fourteen years of age. He did not have much to do with the family.

He would get up at dawn and go to Nagabhushanamgaru's house. He was a *chinna paleru*‡. Feeding the cattle, filling three big pots with water that he had to carry on his shoulders from the west lake, herding the cattle to the fields and then bringing them back, cleaning the cattle shed, carrying messages like 'My dorasanammagoru is going to Gudivada. She wants to know if you would go with her' from his dorasani to another dorasani, or, 'My dora wants Pesadugoru to come as he wants to say something to him urgently' from his dora to another dora … going over to the Komati's§ house to get provisions, going to this one's house or that one's and getting curry leaves or something in return … by the time he finished all such chores and returned home, it would be seven or eight at night. In villages everyone would be half asleep by seven or eight, except in Malapalli. Those who would return home after finishing their tasks for the day would come across others in the bazaars and would enquire about each other's wellbeing. As the chinna palerus would have worked all through the day, they would be so tired they'd be barely awake as they walked.

From the doras' houses on either side of the road, one would hear the warning, 'How will you learn anything if you sleep like a rock right after dinner? … Get up … up … study, sit by the lamp,'

---

* A popular song composed by Tirupati Venkata Kavulu for a play based on the Mahabharata.

† A popular stage actor of the Andhra region known to have sung this song.

‡ The term *paleru* has no exact equivalent term in English. It refers to a person who works under a landlord for a pittance. He is expected to do all kinds of work and is at the beck and call of his master. *Chinna* paleru means young paleru; *pedda* paleru means elder paleru.

§ Komati refers to the Vysya community. They are traditionally a merchant community.

and – '*ka, kaa, ki, kee*.'* The children would memorise, 'Aa ... Ashoka had trees ... had trees planted ... Ashoka had the trees planted.'

Tirapatigadu and his companions would each ape their doras' children and keep walking.

From the Vaishnava priest's house they would hear, '*Yaduvamsha Sudhaambudhi Chandra*'†. They would stop there for a while, and then proceed to walk singing, 'Yaduvamsha Sudhaambudi Chandra'.

In the meanwhile, they would hear a conversation from Kishtaraogaru's house – the mother saying, 'Urinate before you go to bed. If you wet the entire bed like last night, I'll make you sleep next to the dog,' and the boy crying because he had been asked to urinate before going to sleep ...

Even as they sway, walk and laugh noticing everything but pretending not to, Tirapati and other chinna and *pedda* palerus would come back home with a wry face, recollecting all the abuses and beatings they received from their doras and dorasanis.

By the time Tirapati would reach the hut, Sorajjem would be asleep. Tirapati was very fond of his sister. Three children were born after him; all of them died. Sorajjem was born after many years.

Madiga Mary's hut was two huts away from their hut. She sold arrack.

Sorajjem was used to those smells. She was used to pigs too. When the piglets would come near her, she would pull them by their tails.

Bodidi would come out from the next hut. Handing over Sorajjem to Bodidi, Paddalu would go to collect dung.

Sorajjem, Bodidi and four or five other children would go and stand in front of Madiga Mary's arrack shop. Or else, they would go to Bainakodu and watch the pigs playing. Soon, an old woman would come by carrying a basket shouting, 'Puffed rice ... peas ... groundnuts ... sweetmeats ... sesame sweetmeat ...' Then the children would follow the old woman. Unable to tolerate the nuisance of the kids, a woman would help her get the basket down.

---

* *Ka, kaa, ki, kee* refer to the spelling of the letters of the Telugu alphabet.

† Well-known verse from 'Krishna Shabdam', a dance item in the Kuchipudi style.

All the children would stand round the basket. That old woman, some woman, some child would shoo the children away saying, 'Chi, get away from here … hey, move … won't let people buy, won't let them eat …' The children would take three steps back, and then four steps forward. Then it would start again.

In the meanwhile, one of the older girl's mothers would call out, 'Go to Yenkatramaiah's shop and get half *anna** worth of tamarind.' Though the kid would refuse to go initially, after a couple of whacks, she would ask the others, 'Will you come to the Komati's shop with me?'

One of those would ask why she hadn't come when she had asked her earlier.

'Abbo, so far away,' another girl would reply.

'What if you don't come … as if I'm scared! Can't I go by myself?' the girl who had asked them to come would say.

By this time, one of the girls would say, 'I'll come.' A couple of others would now lean this way.

The girl who had asked would say, 'The Komati will give us something, so come along. Let's eat happily.'

Everyone would stop their thoughts and objections, and set out. Some among them would set off in a run … they would reach there.

'Please give half an anna of tamarind.'

'Please give an anna of gingely oil.'

'Please give three *kanees* of onions.'

'Please give a kanee of jaggery.' They would shout and get on Venakatramaiah's nerves. Without looking at them, he would make one bundle after another.

'Won't you please give us something?' the tamarind girl would ask him, and the others too would stretch out their hands. Depending on his mood, Venkatramaiah would give everyone or some of them a few grains of puffed rice or channa dal.

After coming out, they would share what he gave them, and while eating one grain at a time, if something fell down, one would

* *Anna* is a coin equal to roughly six paise of later times. *Arthana* is half an anna. Two annas make a *beda*. Ninety-six *kanees* make one rupee.

say, 'Bhoodevi desired it, don't pick it up,' and another would say, 'We can pick it up, touch our eyes in reverence and eat it.'

The year-and-half girl who would be carried by a six-year old would cry asking for more. While one would say that everyone ought to part with a grain of puffed rice each to pacify her, another would say the sister could give hers to the younger one. Finally, some would give. The elder sister would threaten that she would not help those who had not given now if they were ever in need in the future.

The girl who would return half-an-hour or an hour after she had set out would first be berated with a scream by the mother, 'I wondered which devil snatched you away,' then reprimanded, 'When did you go … when should I cook … when should I take it to your father?' and given two whacks.

That girl would come crying back to these girls. Back to square one.

AFTER HER BIRTH, as she grew up, Sorajjem continued to watch many different kinds of people. But in the recent past, her mouth had stopped closing in astonishment.

The village was being filled with a new environment replete with khaki clothes, with boots, with red topis, with red eyes, with handlebar moustaches, with iron skull caps, with lathis, with guns, with rifles, with deafening sounds as they exercised, with their rushing in and rushing out. Sorajjem did not know that they were the Malabar Police, security guards of the government, famous for their efficiency in eating up the people.

When Sorajjem played with her friends in the mud or in the slush, or with the piglets or the pups, near Madiga Mary's or behind Yakobu's hut, when footsteps like the sound of horses' hooves would ring and bring along the rising dust, people would cry aloud, 'The Malabar people … the police have come!' and then, there would be a silence as if the entire population had cleared out from the village.

Sorajjem would look at the Malabar police through a small hole in their run-down hut, eyes terrified, breath heavy and a face dripping with sweat.

Sorajjem woke up at midnight one day, to chaos and confusion inside their hut, outside the hut and in the entire village. Those police fellows were inside their hut. With glaring eyes, they were questioning Yenkadu about something. Yenkadu was pleading, 'I'm a Mala bastard. What can I know, dora? I don't know, dora.'

'Why would this son of a whore tell us anything just like that?' Saying this, one police fellow gave a blow on Yenkadu's head with a baton.

Sorajjem wailed, 'Ayya.' By then, Paddalu was already standing in a corner and weeping. Then, Brahmamgaru emerged from the crowd, entered the hut saying, 'Don't beat him, Inspectorgaru. He's a good fellow. He'll tell me if I ask him,' and turning towards Yenkadu, said, 'I believe Subbarao came running into Malapalli a little while ago? A number of people saw him. Tell us where he went. Inspectorgaru is a very good man. He has come to save all of us. If you tell him, they'll also reward you. Your photo will also appear in the papers ...'

'Why have you caught me saying Chubbarao, Chubbarao. How do I know who Chubbarao is ...'

'How can you not know Subbarao? Didn't he come from Katuru now and then? Subbarao, Rammurthy, Yenkaiah and a couple of others had come to our village a few times and had even held two or three meetings, didn't they? He has a mole on his cheek. How can you not know? Even a small child of the village knows him.'

'If that is so, why don't you ask them?' said Paddalu.

'Shut up! This has to do with big people from outside. If you think there's no problem and go outside, they'll have both of you, husband and wife, strip your clothes and make you go round the temple. Beware! Don't you know what they did in Yelamarru? ...'

'Why are we bothered about all that, Bemmamgaru? I really don't know anything. What's there that you don't know? Am I the kind to have gone around with Parties and such ... I really haven't seen him. When I was sleeping, you woke me up and asked me ... what will I know? You're my saviour. You have to save me, my wife and my children.' Saying this Yenkadu almost fell at Brahmamgaru's feet.

By then, Sorajjem had gone near her father. and coming in his way, looked fearfully at Brahmamgaru and the police. Brahmamgaru had a wonderful idea. He suddenly pulled Sorajjem, caught hold of her and said, 'Swear on her and say, "I don't know. I haven't seen Subbarao."'

'Really, dora. I swear on my child. I really didn't see him,' said Yenkadu.

'Okay then. Come along Inspectorgaru, I'll have Subbarao found by this time tomorrow,' said Brahmamgaru.

Everyone left.

Then, just as he had promised, in a few days, Brahmam led the police to Subbarao. Subbarao, who refused to surrender to the police, was captured by the entire police force that fired at and killed him in the fields on the bund of Bainakodu. The entire village was left shell-shocked.

Subbaraogaru … Subbaraogaru who had dreamt of wiping out the troubles and tears of the poor … Subbaraogaru who, disturbed by the injustice and violence meted out in Katuru and Yelamarru, had firmly resolved to stand by the poor people … Subbaraogaru who in the struggle in Telangana, in the consciousness that the masses were showing in that struggle, moved by the pains that the people were going through, along with his friends had started the 'Heroic Telangana Struggle Fund' and went around collecting funds from one village to another, awakening the people, making them conscious … who sold off his entire property and gave the amount to the fund … who, even when his wife and children were being crushed in the iron hands of the police, did not turn back but gave up his life to the cause … who, when the police were shooting him to death … had an entire village watch with tears welling up in their eyes.

SUDDENLY ONE DAY, Brahmam descended on Malapalli with his family. Once again, just as at the time of Sorajjem's birth, mikes and records made the village look vibrant.

Brahmam's situation was really good now. Without an expense of even a kanee, his field was being cultivated. From planting to harvesting, three or four bonded labourers would always toil for him.

The fear and hatred that people had for him earlier were no longer there. He had become a great patriot. Someone had written something to that effect in the papers recently.

Brahmam, who had come in a hurry-burry to Malapalli, walked toward Yenkadu's house.

In front of Yenkadu's house, Sorajjem was walking about freely in the bazaars, with her head resembling a palm fruit nibbled by squirrels, an aluminum coin covering her privates, without even a piece of cloth on her body. As soon as Brahmam saw her, he grimaced, turned to his followers and asked, 'Who's this?'

Someone from behind said, 'That's her, Sorajjem.'

'Sorajjem? I don't recognise her!' said Brahmam.

'Yes. We can't recognise her. Look how she is roaming around,' someone said.

Without realising why he was saying this and who he was referring to, Brahmam said, 'Not right. That little rascal, what does she know about manners and such … Till the other day, the white man plundered us. Today we ourselves are … doing to us … *aa* …,' and began to ponder. Coming out of his thoughts, he continued, 'So what? That meant we were plundering ourselves. Plundering doesn't really mean plundering. Means hoarding … That means we would trouble them. Would trouble doesn't really mean would trouble them. Would mean not trouble ourselves. We alone would enjoy. Therefore …' He roared, like the king of the jungle roars when it spots a deer, and turning towards Paddalu, said 'Osey, Paddalu … Put a shirt on her, comb her hair and bring her here. I will make her salute the national flag.'

Paddalu's happiness knew no bounds. A dorasani had given Paddalu a shirt torn to shreds by dogs as she didn't know what to do with it. Though it didn't fit Sorajjem, Paddalu convinced herself it fitted, put it on her, combed back her hair with her finger nails, carried her in her arms and set out, brimming with happiness.

Tirapati came rushing in. 'Don't give Sorajjem to them. They are bloody thieves. Didn't they get Subbaraogaru killed?'

'That's something of the past. Why worry about it now?' Paddalu said, pale with fright.

'Why do you say it's of the past? It's been just two years since the first showers this year. Since then, none of us, paid servants, have been talking to him.'

'Now, hasn't he asked me to bring Sorajjem along?'

'That's why I'm asking you not to.'

'If he asks why I am not sending her, what should I say?'

'Tell him, because you've killed Subbaraogaru.' Yenkadu, who till then had been scratching his legs squatting on the ground, said, 'If you say so, this fellow will call the Malabar police and ask me again what ımy relationship with Chubbarao is ... Don't do such stupid things. What's it to us? Is he going to come every day? Will he salute the flag every day? Take her once a year or once in ten years. What he says is true, but Bemmam will not keep quiet. He is not one of us. If he comes to know that we are thinking like this, he will have us thrown into the cell.'

Paddalu quickly made Sorajjem blow her nose, wiped it with her saree, took her and placed her at Bemmamgaru's feet.

As he unfurled the flag, Brahmamgaru picked up Sorajjem in his arms and made her hold the rope. Sorajjem held on to the rope, and did not let go even when she was asked to, and thus created some confusion. Till a man next to her spanked her on her buttocks.

FOLLOWING HER MOTHER Sorajjem was raising a loud cry, 'Olamma, I too will come.'

Saying no, shouting at her, beating her, Paddalu finally let her daughter follow her.

For a few days, Sorajjem watched her mother work. That's it. Sorajjem's was nothing but a sharp mind. Even when one of the cattle raised its tail to swat flies, she would cry out, 'Olamma, look at this buffalo ... it's lifting it.' Her mother who would have been behind some other buffalo would come running, give her daughter a couple of whacks and go back.

As days went by, Sorajjem stopped following her mother and instead started following her father. When Yenkadu would set out to the moollanka to gather brambles for the stove, Sorajjem would set out too.

'… have to go a long distance, amma. You can come next time,' Yenkadu would say.

'*Oo* … *oo* … I'll come.'

'It's too far …'

'I'll walk … won't ask you to carry me.'

'It's scalding hot … next time, we'll go when it's cool. Come then …'

'*Oo* … *oo* … what's it to me … I'll come.'

'Okay, then … if you say you won't walk, I'll leave you behind there.'

Both father and daughter set out to moollanka when it was scorching hot. In the peak of summer, the heat was hitting hard. Hot winds. As the entire way – with cattle, vehicles and people having continuously trudged along – was filled with thick dust, it was so scalding hot that if you just put your foot on it, the heat would reach your skull. Desiring to walk ahead of her father, Sorajjem ran on the road.

She was confused when she saw Anamaiah who was coming towards them and had stopped. But of course! Anamaiah was no ordinary man. It was a terrifying sight to see a seven-foot man, who was suitably fat for his height and had ears as broad as winnows.

Anamaiah might have been lost in thought, for he asked, 'Whose daughter are you?' When Anamaiah spoke, it sounded as if ten ordinary people were speaking at the same time.

When Sorajjem heard that question, she was totally perplexed. Had a confused expression on her face.

Anamaiah asked loudly, 'Whose daughter are you?' When Anamaiah asked in a loud voice, it appeared as if a hundred people were speaking at the same time.

Sorajjem bawled out.

'What a thing! Why does she cry when I ask her whose daughter she is?' Anamaiah asked Yenkadu who had just arrived there.

'She's my daughter,' said Yenkadu.

'Is she your daughter? Why the hell doesn't she say so?'

'That rascal is just a child, right … she's scared of you.'

'*Ooo*,' he moved away lost in thought.

'When he asked whose daughter are you, why do cry, you idiot? You should say you are so and so's daughter, rather than …' Yenkadu said to his daughter.

Sorajjem nodded, wiping her eyes.

Then the grand journey to moollanka continued. By the time they reached Telagaiahgaru's field, Sorajjem, who had been walking, mumbled, 'Ayya!'

Don't know what world Yenkadu was lost in, he turned and looked at her. Sorajjem appeared as if she had been fried in the sun. Her face had turned red.

'Stupid girl … when I asked you not to come, you protested …' he lifted the girl with both his hands and put her on his shoulders. Sorajjem held on to her father's hair, placed her legs on either side of his neck and sat down. Yenkadu held on to the two feet of his daughter and walked along.

They reached moollanka.

With tumma, seematumma, regu, juvvee, neredu, maredu, gangaravi and palm trees, it looked like a big forest.

Yenkadu put Sorajjem down, and relaxed on the grass saying, 'Lie down for a while. I will lie down too. After getting up I'll break some palm fruit for you.'

'*Ayya*, seematumma fruits!' Sorajjem exclaimed, looking in that direction. 'Look, what big bunches of fruits!' she said running in that direction. The seematumma fruits were hanging within reach of Sorajjem, ripe red.

'Don't eat too much of it. You'll fall sick. Here … don't run like that. There will be thorns. There will be reptiles and such; it's a forest! Stupid girl, where are you going? Sit down for a while … only if you behave yourself will I bring you here again … are you listening?' said Yenkadu.

Would she listen? All kinds of birds, all kinds of trees! And more than anything, bunches of fruits that her hands could reach. Sorajjem was running about here and there and was excited and scared at the same time. A tumma thorn pierced her foot. She gave a maddening shriek, '*Ayyo*.' Yenkadu was shaken at the thought that a snake might have bitten her.

Sorajjem could not balance herself on one leg and fell down. Yenkadu placed her grimy tiny foot on his lap and pulled out the thorn effortlessly with his hands that were rough and coarse, reflecting the hard work he had done all his life. As drops of blood oozed out, he rubbed hard and wiped them with his spit.

Later, he found a leaf, squeezed its juice, applied it on the wound along with a bit of leaf and tied a bandage with a blade of grass.

'Did you listen when I asked you to sit down? … No … as if you ever listen to me … That's why I asked you not to come. Why would you listen? Now look. Don't know how deep the thorn went in. At least now, sit down and don't move about …' Saying this, he carried Sorajjem and set her down under another tree.

It was evening. Far away, bullock carts were coming from the village and from Karimerla. The bells around the bulls' necks were tinkling as if they were setting out to work.

Perhaps the heat had abated a bit, the farmers were taking manure to the fields.

Yenkadu was was cutting the brambles with a sickle.

'*Ayyayyo*,' Sorajjem shrieked. She had tried to walk.

'Don't walk. It will bleed.'

'No … I have my slippers on … no, no … boots … I found them there,' said Sorajjem thrilled looking at her feet.

Yenkadu looked at Sorajjem's feet. Sorajjem had put on red-and-white-striped palm spathes on her feet like slippers and was going about dragging them.

'Osey, stupid child! There will be scorpions in them. Did you check before wearing them?' Yenkadu was agitated.

'They aren't there,' said Sorajjem.

For a while she went around hobbling.

After a while, she came slowly to her father and asked, 'Why don't you get real slippers stitched for me?'

'Why now?'

'*Aa* … my feet will not scorch if I wear slippers … I'll come with you every day.'

'What will you do?'

'I'll collect brambles.'

'My wonderful girl … all right. I'll get them stitched for you …'

'*Ooo*, I want them right now!'

'Where can I get them now? Will they fall from the heavens? Once we go back home, don't you know Madiga Mary's brother, I'll ask him … I'll take you along … you have to give your measurements … okay?'

'*Ooo* …' Sorajjem was whining. Yenkadu made a small bundle of the brambles. Placed it on his head.

'Will you walk?'

'*Oo* …'

He took hold of one of Sorajjem's hands and started to walk slowly. Sorajjem saw a palm tree and said, 'Ayya, you told me you would pluck some palm fruits for me.'

Yenkadu set down his bundle.

He lifted his head towards the palm fruits and saying, 'These are too ripe,' he went and stood beneath another palm tree. Saying, 'These are just right,' he took his towel, tied it round his feet like a ring, held the sickle in his mouth and swiftly climbed up the tree. He shouted from up high, 'Go far away, out there … there underneath that tree …'

Sorajjem stood far away and kept looking at the palm tree.

Yenkadu very deftly cut two bunches. Even before the bunches touched the ground, the fruits fell off from the bunches and dropped to the ground – *chat* … *chat* …

Yenkadu slid down the tree quickly. Having got down, he collected those fruits Sorajjem had failed to collect, cut them so that the kernels were visible, and saying, 'Eat quickly … don't waste the water in them. Here, drink this …' he handed tiny little ones to her.

He too ate the kernels of four or five unripe fruits quickly and said, 'Come, let's go now.'

'Let's take some home …'

'Okay, take these two.' Saying this, he picked up the ears, tied them in such a manner that they could be held in her hands.

Sorajjem took them saying, 'This is for amma, this is for annayya.'

'Then, what about you …'

'I've eaten already, right …'

They were walking towards the village. They met Anamaiah again on their way back.

'Hey, Yenka, what's your daughter saying?' he questioned in his ten-throated voice.

'Now ask her, dora, see how she replies.'

'Hey you …' Anamaiah said.

'Don't be scared. Tell him whatever he asks you,' said Yenkadu.

'Whose daughter are you?' asked Anamaiah laughing.

'I'm so and so's daughter,' said Sorajjem confidently.

'Whose daughter are you?' he asked in his twenty-five throated voice.

'I'm so and so's daughter,' Sorajjem said yet again, confidently.

Yenkadu set his bundle down and held his stomach. 'Curse you! I said, if anyone asks you, you should say, "I'm so and so's daughter."'

Anamaiah gave a thousand-throated laughter.

By the time they reached the village, it was getting dark. They met Amaraiah at the bridge.

'Who's that?' he asked. Without waiting for an answer, he said, 'Where are the brambles from?'

'From moollanka … that's filled with thorny brambles …'

'*Ooo* … but whose are the palm fruits?'

'Ours,' said Sorajjem, hiding the fruits behind her back.

'Is this bitch your daughter?'

'Yes, dora …'

'She looks nice and round.'

'All due to your blessing.'

'From whose trees?'

'Not yours.'

'Who do they belong to, you son of a whore? If they are mine, won't I pound your bones?' Laughter still shone on Amaraiah's face.

'Why such words for just palm fruits, dora … If you say such things what will become of Mala sons of whores like us …'

'You are shaken just by words? … Don't pluck from our trees. My son-in-law and children in Madras have written that they are coming here. If there are no fruits when they come, I'll have to go looking for them elsewhere …'

'Don't I know that? Our Ganganamma's palm tree has a bounty of fruits. Who has the energy to pluck them? As the child was crying … I cut a bunch that had only five fruits. And that too, not of the people from our village. The tree belongs to the people of Karimella.'

'Okay, go.'

'Where are you going at this dark hour?'

'Just here … to the road.'

'I'll get going, dora.'

'Okay, go.'

By the time they reached home, Paddalu had returned after walking around fields far and near.

'When I wanted to cook rice, there was not a drop of water. Throw that bundle down, take the two pots on the sling and quickly get two loads of water. I can't take this any more today,' she moaned.

Yenkadu threw the bundle down and grumbled.

'Okay, get one load of water. I won't disturb you till the meal is ready.'

'Okay, throw the pots here.' Saying this Yenkadu set the loops of the sling right and set out.

Moonlight shone white – on Malapalli too, for moonlight came from the sky. Otherwise, the doras would perhaps have not let it enter Malapalli.

All the Mala children were playing 'moonlight-shade' in the moonlight.

Sorajjem, Bodidi and her brother, Sankurattirigadu were playing along with the other children in the moonlight.

When Bodidi's mother called out, and the two went away. Sorajjem too came into the hut. Sorajjem sat on her haunches near the stove, looked at the boiling rice, sat near her mother, placed her head on her mother's lap, and asked, 'Why doesn't the moonlight come every day, amma?'

'Does it come every day anywhere?'

'No, but why doesn't it come?'

'It doesn't, that's it. Elders say … some days of moonlight and some days of darkness. Can it be according to our wish?'

Sorajjem was perplexed, and looked at her mother. She muttered, 'It'll be good if it comes every day.'

'Stupid girl! There will be moonlight on full moon days. There will be darkness on new moon days. That's all …'

Meanwhile, Ratti had come in.

'Paddakka, can you give me two dry chillies?'

'Wait, let me check.' Saying this, Paddalu made Sorajjem get up from her lap, went in, got a few chillies and enquired, 'Is your mother-in-law able to get up?'

'*Aaa* … as if she will get up … my ill luck, her ill luck.'

'Has she any energy left?'

'Where will she have the energy? She conceived fourteen children and threw them out into the world. Not all of them survived. Nothing seems to be going well for some time now. We want to take her to the hospital … when we don't have enough to eat, how much can we spend on doctors and medicines? Your brother-in-law had the Mangali doctor give her a few tablets. That sure as hell is not going to cure her …'

'That's true. How can she survive when her time is up? All of us have to go to the graveyard either today or tomorrow. For a few days, this way and that; she sure as hell is not going to live …'

'That's it, that's it … I'll get going, akka.' Saying this, Ratti left.

In the moonlight it appeared as if flour had been spread out. Yenkadu was lying down on a mat. Turning this way and that, he finally lay down on his stomach and said, 'Amma, Sorajjem, please scratch my back. It's been itching a lot.'

Sorajjem was lying on her back next to Yenkadu and was looking at the moon that was rushing towards the clouds.

'Ayya, where does the moon live?'

'Amma … osey … scratch my back a bit.'

Sorajjem turned towards her father. Yenkadu's body was dark but the parts where he had the itch were white. Sorajjem started to rub Yenkadu's back with her tiny hands.

'Scratch with your nails, amma.'

When Sorajjem scratched once with her nails, her nails were filled with mud. She removed mud from the rest of the fingers with her thumb and the mud from the thumb with her middle finger.

'Scratch …'

'… all this is mud!'

'Would there be gold on people who toil in the mud?' Paddalu said coming out from inside the hut.

'Oh, you've come? Sit here and scratch properly. This chit of a girl has no strength,' Yenkadu said.

'*Oo* ... here,' Paddalu scratched his back so hard that the skin would have peeled off, and said, 'How humid, I have never sweated so much. I'll lie down for a while. Ramudammagaru asked me to come early tomorrow morning.' Having said this, she placed her head on the mat and lay down on the floor.

'Why?'

'Why, you ask? Isn't the day after day-after-tomorrow Somaiahgaru's death anniversary?'

'Is it really the day after day-after-tomorrow? ... the great man had no strength in his hands.'

'*Aa* ... he didn't. It is said that a dead man has large eyes ... this man would only ogle at women.'

'*Aa* ... as if there are men who don't ogle at women!'

'You ought to be ashamed. You are justifying him.'

'*Oo* ... amma ... my whole body seems to be on fire ... Sorajjem, are you asleep?'

'No, ayya.'

'Hold on to my stick and stamp on my legs.'

'Abba, the slip of a girl will fall down ... It'll go away on its own, if only you have a wink of sleep,' Paddalu said, and turned to a side to sleep.

'I won't fall down ... I'll hold on tightly to the stick ... ayya, wait, I'm coming.'

Holding on to the stick, Sorajjem slowly got on to Yenkadu's legs, and started to walk on both the legs.

'Amma ... go back ... back ... *aa* ... there. Stamp ... really well ... *aa*.'

Sorajjem was jumping on Yenkadu's legs and thinking.

'Ayya.'

'What's it?'

'Where do people who die live?'

'Why do you want to know that now? ... They'll go either to hell or heaven.'

'You said they'll burn them. How will they go?'

'Even if you burn them, they'll go. Going doesn't mean going with this body. There's a light within. That'll go. You can't understand all that now. You'll know all that when you grow older.'

'Do you know?' Paddalu teased him.

'*Aa* ... why don't I know?'

'Where will Somaiahgaru go?'

'Somaiahgaru will go to heaven.'

'*Aa* ... why won't he? He must be roasting in hell by now,' said Paddalu with animosity.

'No, no. That great man will go only to heaven. How many poojas had he got performed? Will all of that go waste? What do you know? Stupid one!'

'*Aa*, you'll come to know. Do you know that he is supposed to have poisoned and killed his three wives?'

'He'll do with his wives what he wants to. There's no connection between that and this.'

'Why do you say that?' Paddalu asked mockingly.

'His birth as a *Bembadu**, of course!'

'I believe all are equal before god!'

'How can all be equal? Even if all were equal, *Bemballu* have a different route.'

Sorajjem stopped stamping on her father's legs and lay down.

The moon did not stop rushing through the sky. It kept running its race with the clouds.

LIKE EVERY DAY, Sorajjem, Sankurattirigadu and Bodidi got ready by the time food was offered to god in the Rama temple.

The priest would give a fistful of *vadapappu*† and two or three pieces of coconut to the older people; by the time he came to the children, he would give two grains of vadapappu and a tiny coconut piece.

* Brahmin

† *Vadapappu* is soaked and salted moong dal (*pesallu*) offered to god.

That day too he dropped a few grains from high above into their cupped hands.

Like she did every day, Bodidi asked, 'Give us a little more.'

'Did you think this was a meal, to eat it the way you eat rice – a snack, god's prasadam,' scolded the priest, and threw a tiny morsel to each one.

Ponnammagaru came out of the temple muttering, 'Rama, Rama.' Seventy-two years ago, her father sold her to an eighty-year-old man in the name of marriage for eight rupees.

Ponnamma was then six years old. Ponnamma's husband died when he was in his eighty-third year. Ponnamma became a widow at nine. Since then, she lived only with her faith in Rama. Now she was seventy-eight. She would say she could not see anything at all, but still she would wear spectacles.

It was pitch dark outside. Sorajjem, Sankurattirigadu and Bodidi were cursing the priest who had given them very little of the snack.

Ponnammagaru noticed them.

Calling out, 'Osey, Sorajjem,' and calling out to Rama too – 'Rama, Rama' – she got down two steps, and handed over her burden to the Mala children saying, 'Take me to my house … amma … Rama, Rama.' Rama could not bear her burden any moment, but she would insist there was no one for her in this world other than Rama.

Sorajjem and the others were used to this. It also made them happy. Ponnamma would treat them a little kindly. They knew that when they dropped her home, she would give them a piece of coconut.

The three of them held Ponnammagaru's stick on one side as she walked on the other.

'Slowly, slowly … why such hurry … Rama, Rama!'

They were indeed in a hurry till the coconut piece fell into their hands. 'Ponnammagaru, can't you see?' asked Sankurattirigadu.

'If I could see, would I let you hold my stick? I would have twirled the stick at you if you had come near, Rama, Rama.'

'If you can't see, why the glasses?'

The children giggled.

'Oh, may your stomach burn with hunger …'

'Maybe with the glasses, she can see a bit,' said Sorajjem.

'Osey, may your stomach boil! You're a clever one.'

'If you have glasses, how can you not see?' said Sankurattirigadu.

'*Aa*, she can see,' Bodidi scolded her younger brother.

She was scared that Ponnammagaru would get angry and deny them the coconut piece.

'*Aa* … I can't see if I have them on. I can't see if I don't have them on. Rama, Rama.'

'Then why those?'

'Rama, Rama, don't irritate me.'

They reached Ponnammagaru's house.

Climbing the steps of the verandah, she said, 'Amma … Rama, Rama. Here. Break the shell and eat the pieces … don't touch me, you Mala bitches.'

They broke the shell and shared the pieces.

Ponnammagaru was exhausted and squatted on the steps. 'Everything is Rama's play, Rama's play.'

'What does Rama's play mean?'

'Maybe Rama has a whistle,' said Sorajjem.

'Wait. Ponnammagaru, does Rama whistle?'

'Orey, you'll become blind. Slap your cheeks to say sorry.'

'Why did you lose your eyesight?'

Seventy-eight-year-old Ponnamma was exhausted. Unable to answer the questions of the Mala children, she sighed, 'Rama, Rama … Somehow you've ensured that I reached home, dear Rama.'

'We are the ones who brought you home, why do you say it's Rama?' asked Bodidi.

'We are the ones who brought you, right?' Sorajjem too added.

'How could you do that, Mala bitches? It's all Rama. Go away, it's getting late.'

'Then why did you ask us to bring you home?'

'Will you go or won't you?' Saying this she twirled her stick and beat it on the steps.

The children jumped far away and went into the street laughing.

NOW, SORAJJEM STOPPED going behind her mother or father.

After the bundling of the paddy was done in the fields, she would go along with other Mala children to collect the paddy grains that had fallen off. Bodidi and she were a good duo. They would gather the fallen paddy grains in slushy fields as well as in dry fields. They would compete with each other as to who would gather more. Even though he was young, Sankurattirigadu too would gather in the same manner as they did.

That year Sorajjem had gathered well.

Moving his eyes up and down, Sankurattirigadu said, 'With the paddy grains I have gathered I will buy myself a new shirt.' Sorajjem and Bodidi too thought of buying shirts for themselves.

At that moment, slippers came to Sorajjem's mind.

'I'll buy slippers,' she said.

'Then I'll buy anklets for my feet,' said Bodidi.

It had been quite a while since the bundling of paddy. The farmers thought of planting minumu or pesaru or pilli pesaru* or jute as a second crop. The farmers did not keep quiet when they spotted children on the fields as they felt they were stamping the fields.

Sorajjem had her mother weigh the paddy she had gathered over a month.

When each measure was weighed, Sorajjem felt that the paddy ought not to lessen. Finally, the entire lot of paddy was done.

Paddalu said it measured sixteen *marakalu*†.

'Is it a sack full?' asked Sorajjem.

'A sack full? … Twenty-six marakalu make a sack full.'

Sorajjem ran to inform Bodi. Bodi too had had her paddy weighed.

'Mine was sixteen marakalu,' said Sorajjem.

'Mine was eighteen, my brother's thirteen.'

Sorajjem thought it would have been good if she too had a younger brother.

'Both of you together have more,' said Sorajjem with an upset face.

---

* Minumu, pesaru and pilli pesaru are different kinds of pulses.

† One *maraka* is equivalent to two *seers*, which is approximately two kilograms.

'Osey, Sorajjem, my mother snatched away our paddy, you know,' said Bodi, with a sad face.

'Why?' Sorajjem was shocked.

'Because my mother snatched away the paddy, my brother has run away.'

'Why?' Sorrajem asked again.

'We thought of buying shirts or something, isn't it? "The Komati will cheat you. I'll sell it for you," saying this, mother took away our paddy, sat on Raghavulu's cart that was going that way and went to Komati's shop. I believe she will take the money,' Bodidi cried.

Sorajjem felt very bad, wondering if there could be such injustice in the world.

'Where did Sankurattirigadu go?' she asked.

'He went on the Mallayapalem road.'

'Come, let's go get him.'

Bodi set out, as if she was waiting for just those very words.

When they went a distance on the Mallayapalem road, they found Sankurattirigadu playing gilli danda with the boys who were tending the cattle.

When they asked him to come, he refused. When they asked, 'Where will you go?' he said, 'Somewhere.' When they asked, 'Where will you stay when it gets dark?' he softened a bit. Moreover, it had been a long time since they set out.

'If my money is given back to me, I'll come.'

'She'll give, don't worry.'

The three returned and came into the village.

By the time Sorajjem came home, Paddalu was not there. When she looked for her paddy, she found the vessels empty. Sorajjem was terribly upset.

When she saw her mother she wept copiously, 'Where's my paddy?'

'Osey, stupid child! Thieves haven't taken it away. I took it and sold it to the Komati. You got eight rupees,' Paddalu said, wiping her daughter's tears. She placed three sugar candies in her palm.

'You must buy me slippers,' said Sorajjem.

'You can buy them.'

Bodi and Sankurattirigadu's mother too gave the same explanation to them.

Though Paddalu had sold the paddy, the Komati did not give her even a kanee. He set it off against her loan. Paddalu pleaded with the Komati and got the sugar candies. With Bodi's mother too, the same.

When the kids asked for money, the mothers would say, 'We'll give tomorrow ... tomorrow,' and four months went by.

Sorajjem did not have slippers.

Bodi did not have anklets.

Her brother did not have shirts.

Later, the mothers said, 'This time, you keep the money you get from the fallen grains of paddy.'

They thought, 'We'll buy them from this time's fallen grains of paddy.' They counted, 'There's still six months to go.'

SORAJJEM, CARRYING THE bundle of food, stopped near an opening at a field bund.

Paddalu, who had asthmatic cough and slept god-knows-when, had got up very late that morning.

It was very late in the morning. They had started transplanting in the fields a few days ago. Paddalu, thinking of the abuses showered by the doras on the coolies who came late, washed a fistful of rice in a hurry, lit the fire, threw the rice into a pot, asked the girl to take care of it, and ran to the fields, even as she was tying her hair into a knot.

Sorajjem sat for a while in front of the stove, pushed the brambles this way and that, boiled the broken rice to a lump, kept it in a vessel, threw a bit of chilli paste into it, bundled the vessel with a cloth and set out.

When she saw water gushing out of the opening at the field bund, she was fascinated and stood looking at it. The water in the channel, with a soft sound, was inviting the grass on the other side of the bund too to go along, and pulling it along, was running towards the fields.

Sorajjem slowly got into the opening, leaving the bundle on the bund. The water came up to her knees. The water was twirling round her feet and running. Sorajjem played for quite a while in the water when a swamp snake lifted its head searching for its prey. No sooner did Sorajjem spot the snake, than she jumped in two leaps on to the bund, placed the food bundle on her head and began to walk only on the bund.

All the fields were ploughed and watered. The fields which were levelled after furrowing and kept ready for transplanting appeared like shining glass. The fields seemed as though they were filled with clouds as the palm trees were swaying with their heads bent towards the fields.

If there were small mounds of mud here and there, crows and storks had got on to them and were making a feast of the insects there. The landlords were going along the bunds and screaming at the women coolies.

All the women coolies had hitched up their sarees to their knees and tucked them at their back, and were planting the seedlings, bending down and walking back quickly.

Sorajjem went over the bunds in the middle of the expansive fields, and looking at the coolies planting the seedlings, at the doras bossing over them, and at the shadows of the trees on the water in the fields, reached the field where her mother worked.

Paddalu had not eaten the previous night as she had been unwell. As soon as she saw her daughter she shouted, 'What were you doing all this while?'

Sorajjem stood without uttering a word.

'Why don't you speak? Where the hell were you all this while?'

'As there was an opening in the field there ...'

'If there was an opening ... did you get stuck there? ... you wretched thing.'

When the coolies came out from the field, Paddalu gave a couple of knocks with her knuckles on her daughter's head.

Sorajjem ran along the bund crying.

'Wait, I'll break your legs.' Saying this Paddalu ran behind her daughter, but the other coolies calmed her down shouting, 'Let her be. Why bother with her?'

WHEN THE CIRCUS came near the big school, Sorajjem ran there and stood gaping at the bears and the monkeys.

Bodi and Sankurattirigadu were rushing into the village.

'Oley, Bodi, oley Sankurattiriga, come, let's see the bear, come,' screamed Sorajjem.

Hearing Sorajjem's scream, they stopped running and came to her, weeping.

Sorajjem who was agog with enthusiasm had a sad face noticing them cry, and asked, 'Why?'

'I believe they have tied my elder brother to a tree and are going to beat him up,' Bodidi said, and started running again. Sankurattirigadu too ran behind her, crying.

Sorajjem waited for a second and then she too ran behind them.

Jojigadu was older than Bodi and Sankurattirigadu. Their father died in the fields when the bullock cart overturned, six months after Sankurattirigadu was born. When he died, he was working as a paleru with Nallachantabbayigaru.

Jojigadu was eight when his father died. His mother made him work at Nallachantabbayigaru's house as a chinna paleru. She would do coolie work, and go now and then to Kamma houses to swab their floors, pound rice and make dung cakes.

Some would show pity on her because she was a 'widow, who lost her husband'.

By the time Bodidi, Sankurattirigadu and Sorajjem reached the tamarind tree in front of Nallachantabbayigaru's house, many doras were standing there.

Sovigaru, who was going that way in a bullock cart, enquired, 'What happened, Peddada?'

'Nothing really … the Mala fellow seems to have stolen something in Chantannayyagaru's house. They have tied him to a tree,' Peddadu said.

'Thrash him with slippers, that son of a whore, so he won't do it again,' even as Sovigaru was saying this, his cart turned the corner.

'Must break the hands of this thief son of a whore,' said Mohanaraogaru who was there.

'Arey, Pesadu, why waste time unnecessarily? Go, get a *veesa*[*] of sugar, tie his hands and feet, throw him on the ground, pour sugar on him, and sprinkle a few drops of water. The son of a whore must learn a lesson that will last many births … go, get it … *oo* …' said Malleswararaogaru.

Sundaraiahgaru who was going in a hurry came there, and said addressing everyone, 'What did this fellow do?'

'It seems he has stolen,' said three or four in one voice. All of them would only say, 'It seems.'

'Not even the size of the little finger, this son of an ass. Will he listen when he grows up? He will become a king of robbers in the entire Gudivada taluk. Look at his eyes, this wretched fellow's eyes are the eyes of a thief. Gore the thief son of a whore with *kattavalu*[†],' he said, and began to leave, but returned to abuse, 'You, son of a whore,' and suddenly threw himself on him and slapped him on both his cheeks. Jojigadu, who till then had controlled his tears in his yam-like face, burst into tears. As soon as she heard him cry, his mother started wailing loudly. Jojigadu's sister, brother and Sorajjem too started to cry.

All the doras got angry at the same time.

'Hey, you, stop those false tears. Wretched tears,' they screamed.

All of them controlled their tears.

Leaving in a rush, Sundaraiahgaru stopped at the turning of the lane and screamed, 'Don't let go the thief son of an ass. Make a pulp of his hands and legs and then let him go. Let's see who the son of an ass will complain to,' and turned round the corner.

On hearing those words, Bodidi, Sankurattirigadu and Sorajjem started crying again.

'Pesadubabu, please let him off just this once, babu. I'll die and be born in your stomach. He's not the kind to steal, *nayannayana* …' Jojigadu's mother was pleading, falling at the feet of one and all.

'That means?' Nallachantabbayigaru said, his eyes widening in anger. 'Have I done it and put the blame on him? … you thief of a whore, it is you, not he that I should kick, I should tie you to a tree,

---

[*] One *veesa* is approximately 1.5 kilograms.

[†] *Kattavalu* are triangular-shaped spades.

you slut …' saying this, he jumped all over her fuming with rage, 'Arey, Mohana, go to the shed and get a rope, let's tie him up and flog him. Then he will tell us if he has stolen or not.'

Mohanarao went quickly to the shed and brought a thick rope.

They untied Jojigadu from the tree and hung him from a branch. Two or three held the other end of the rope and pulled. As the rope was tied round his belly, he felt suffocated. He was screaming, writhing in pain. The mother slumped to the ground. She was unconscious. The children surrounded her and were screaming and crying.

Pesadubabu looked this way and that, brought dried grass and put it underneath the branch. Someone brought kerosene oil and poured enthusiastically on the grass. Mohanarao set fire to the grass. It burned.

They kept pulling Jojigadu from the other side of the branch so that the fire neither touched nor burnt him.

Some among the doras said, 'Stop it, that's enough,' and went away hurriedly, leaving the job to the youngsters.

In the meanwhile someone came running and whispered something into Nallachantabbayi's ears. Now he was like a monkey on hot coal.

'*Aa.* Ask him to come, no matter which son of a whore. Arey, Pesadu, get our youngsters together. It seems all the Mala sons of whores are coming with sticks. Let's see how far this will go, are you listening? Here, go get some more kerosene oil and pour it all over him. Let's see what those sons of whores will do,' saying this, he jumped all over.

Jojigadu's mother regained consciousness, and ran here and there in a frenzy.

'Babu, ayya, I'll catch hold of your legs … please save my son … ayya, ayya,' she fell at everyone's feet.

Bodidi, Sankurattirigadu and Sorajjem were sobbing uncontrollably. Pesadu hurriedly went into the house, brought a bottleful of kerosene and poured it over Jojigadu. Some of it fell in the fire below and the fire became even bigger. The flames flared up, spread to the kerosene oil on Jojigadu's body.

Jojigadu was aflame.

The mother ran quickly, hugged her son and fell unconscious.

Bodidi, Sankurattirigadu and Sorajjem stopped crying, stood horrified, staring like insane people.

The rope that was tied around Jojigadu broke, and he fell to the ground with a thud. By then, Jojigadu was dead. From tying Jojigadu to the tree, all of this happened within a quarter of an hour. When people realised he was dead, one by one they slipped away.

In the meanwhile, Malas and Madigas came running from Malapalli and the fields.

Except for Jojigadu's mother, Bodi, Sankurattirigadu and Sorajjem, no one else was there.

All those who came were furious.

Some ran to Gudivada police station.

Some stood guarding the corpse with thick sticks.

The police arrived even before it grew dark.

That case went on for six months. Nallachantabbayi sold an acre of his land. They threw four youth from Malapalli into prison for killing Jojigadu at the field bund because of a fight.

GOING BEHIND CATTLE with a dung basket to collect dung, jumping into wild grass and bushes to collect thorny brambles, roaming about in the fields in the sun and rain – these were no longer pleasurable for Sorajjem.

When Sorajjem saw school-going children carry slates, books and bags, and go to school across the lake bund, she too felt like going to school.

Once they reach the school, the school master saying 'mother', 'cow', 'house', 'fly' and the children screaming those words in unison, the children running out enthusiastically when the interval bell and the lunch bell rang – all these appeared exciting and enjoyable to Sorajjem.

She told her father she wanted to go to school.

Yenkadu had recently learnt a whimsical laugh. Whatever any one asked him he would laugh that laugh.

If his wife said, 'There is no broken rice. Go, somehow, get from somewhere, a small amount of broken rice,' he would laugh as if to ask, 'What need of broken rice?'

'What's that wretched laugh? It doesn't matter if there's no broken rice, but don't laugh that wretched laugh,' Paddalu would scream.

Sometime ago, Tirapati had said, 'Orey, ayya, I can't do this paleru's job any more. The doras are taking the lives out of us. Go get one or two acres from somewhere. Let's cultivate it and live.'

Yenkadu had laughed hysterically at this.

'Acres … he says acres. Where are the acres? With what will you cultivate?' Yenkadu had slumped on the string cot and laughed for a long while.

Tirapati had only recently begun to see and understand the world clearly. His grandfathers were palerus. His father too was a paleru. He too was a paleru. If he got married tomorrow, his sons too would be palerus. Grandsons too, palerus.

In the entire Malapalli only five or six had fields. And that too how much? – an acre or an acre and a half. Only Durgadu had two acres – a great property! One who had a bit of things, got it by licking the arse of that dora or this dora; it was not possible for wretched people otherwise.

His father's words, 'With what will you cultivate?' made Tirapati very dispirited.

After witnessing Jojigadu's murder, there was some change in the way many Mala, Madiga youth thought. Tirapati was the first among them.

It was only after this that the youth started to get together at the Mala Ramulori temple in the evening, after they finished their work at their doras' houses, and think about the injustices that were taking place.

That's why he told his father that he wanted to give up being a paleru and do something independently, and his father laughed out hysterically.

'He seems to have gone crazy, amma,' Tirapati told Paddalu.

'Perhaps … it seems like that to me too. Has this wretched fate too fallen on us, O God!' Saying this, Paddalu heaved a heavy sigh.

'I'll go to school.'

'... you wretched one! Do you think you are a dora's child? What will you do going to school? Will you become a teacher? Will you become a nurse? Osey, may your stomach burn!' Saying this, he kept thinking of it and laughed.

Sorajjem was terrified and did not think of school for a few days.

Again, one day when her mother returned home she muttered, 'Olamma, send me to school.'

When her daughter asked that, Paddalu's sorrow suddenly burst out. She held her daughter close, cried and kept quiet.

The husband ... had lost his mind and was roaming about. The son ... was having problems with the doras. Herself ... had asthmatic cough. How then schooling for the wretch of a girl?

Even if she wanted to send her to school was that so easy? Had to buy clothes. Had to buy books. The girl was already into her eighth year. If she placed her in the house of someone like Anasuyamma, she could lead her own life.

'Why do people like us who live by doing coolie work need schooling? Will that give you food or anything else?' she said, cajoling her daughter.

Sorajjem became disheartened listening to her mother's words. Her hope turned towards her brother.

That day she sat up without sleeping till her brother returned. Tirapati came after nine.

'Orey annayya, why didn't you study?' she asked her brother as he stepped in.

'Why are you asking me now?'

'Tell me,' she asked affectionately.

'How could I study? Did your mother and father let me study?'

'If that is so, orey annayya, why don't you educate me? I will get higher degrees like our teacher and then have you educated.'

Without being conscious of it, Sorajjem uttered those words, infusing all her life into them. That's why Tirapati took them not as sweet words uttered by his sweet sister, but thought about them seriously.

'Okay. I'll educate you,' he said most decisively.

Next morning as soon as he got up, Tirapati told his mother, 'Olamma, from today we must send Sorajjem to school. Don't say this and that but send her.'

'Stop that nonsense, have you gone mad? Why does she need education, does she need to take up a job, rule the land?' said Paddalu.

'You mother– … with such wretched words, you ruined my life. If only I had studied, I would have had a job by now, in Bezawada or some other place.'

'*Aa, aa*, yes you'd do that. All the educated people in the entire village are employed, aren't they? Even so, are you born to a rich farmer or a Kamma dora? Saying education, education, you quarrel with me. If only both of you were destined to study, you'd have been born in some great one's house.'

Paddalu had thought of educating her son when he was young. She also dreamt that her son would work in the taluk office like Siromani's brother. As her son grew up, year after year, she dreamt that her son was born and was growing up only to get educated, get a job and help the family come out of the paleru legacy of his father and forefathers, the coolie fate bestowed on them.

By the time he was old enough to go to school, she had had two more, and time was spent in the frenzy of rituals related to childbirth, in the wailing and moaning at their death and her own ill-health.

She hardened her heart thinking that if she thought of tomorrow's job, they wouldn't have enough to eat at present, and unwilling to throw a stone in his bowl, she finally made him a chinna paleru in Nagabhushanamgaru's house when he was six or seven, hoping, 'He will at least get some food.'

He too did not make a hue and cry that he wanted to go to school. Once when he went up to the school window as he was playing, they abused him saying, 'Mala son of a whore, get out,' and after that Tirapati never stepped even into its shadow.

After she placed her son as a paleru, Paddalu was unable to swallow even a morsel of food … Paddalu had seen from her childhood how children from Malapalli became palerus at the age of five or six. Even then she did not have the stomach to bear the fact that her son was toiling hard.

When she passed by their house sometime and saw her son's tiny little hands wash dirty dishes or his tiny little feet sweep the urine pits in the cattle shed or his teeny-weeny eyes shed tears because of the dirt and dust falling into them, she felt miserable. As days went by, she got used to all of this.

'How can anyone born to a Mala whore find happiness? They will be what they are destined to be,' thinking so, she left him to his fate. She swallowed her misery and remained silent.

When Sorajjem embraced Paddalu a few days ago and said, 'I want to study,' Paddalu was about to place her dormant hopes on Sorajjem. She thought, 'Perhaps, she will become a teacher like Krupavati. But … the days … but the days … what kind of days are these? The young bitch may want it … but if on a day, the girl did not bring the brambles, let alone what goes over the fire, the fire below would not be on. Not just that, a week ago Anasuyamma had asked, "Paddalu, will you send this one to work?"'

And when Paddalu had replied, 'She's the one to make the food when I go for coolie work,' she had said, 'Okay then, but send her at least by the time the produce is collected.'

Knowing that nothing much will be gained by keeping the girl in the hut just to cook a seer of grain, Paddalu decided to send Sorajjem to work soon.

'If we send her to work, she will lead her own life. What will she get if we admit her in school? How many years she'll have to study? How will the household run?' Paddalu thought carefully and said no to Sorajjem studying.

Now that Tirapati was adamant about getting her educated, she relented, 'We don't know what she is destined to do,' and with hope in her heart, 'He's saying he'll educate her. Let's see,' she added, 'Do you want me to ask the Brahmin to look for an auspicious day?'

'A good day is one in which a good deed is done. All days are the same. There are no good days or bad days among them,' said Tirapati.

He was proud that he would get his sister highly educated. As for Sorajjem, one could guess … Once she knew her mother had agreed, she ran fast to Bodi and told her.

'Osey, Bodi, I'm going to go to school. Don't you know the big school, I'm going there. From today itself. My brother asked me to.' When she said this in excitement and happiness, throwing her hands high up in the air and twisting them, Bodi stood open-mouthed unable to fathom.

'Then, who'll collect the brambles for your house?' asked her brother.

'Don't know, perhaps my mother will gather them.'

'Doesn't your mother have to collect dung? How will she collect the brambles?'

Sorajjem turned back without answering them.

Tirapati took Sorajjem to the big school.

Sorajjem had a slate and a piece of slate pencil in her hand.

Paddalu made her wear the least torn among the gowns she had. She also cleaned her hair a bit.

Tirapati knew all the teachers in the school quite well.

Annapoorna Sastrigaru saw him and asked him in a typically Brahmin manner, 'Yera, Tirapatiga, what's it? Why have you come here?'

Tirapati, feeling a bit shy, but with a lot of humility, said, 'This is my younger sister. I brought her along to admit her in this school.'

Annapoorna Sastri laughed at him scornfully.

'What times have befallen us? Mala bitch of a whore, what, they too want education! That's why they call this *kali kalam*[*]. Even so, education for a bitch of a girl? If you educate bitches, can we control them? Go away, go, why does she need education? Take her away. Take her and put her somewhere where she can work. She'll at least get a few morsels.' He thus advised him – on behalf of all castes that were well-fed.

Tirapati was incensed. By then, Sorajjem was completely disheartened. She thought they might not admit her in school.

'Pontulugoru, the other day, while hoisting the flag, Bemmamgaru said, women and men, Mala and Madiga, must all study,' Tirapati said calmly.

---

[*] *Kali kalam* refers to the present times which are bad compared to the previous eras.

'Brahmamgaru? Did he say so? Okay then, go in from the other side and meet Somayajulugaru.' Sastri said and left, with his mouth open and twirling his tongue over his teeth.

Somayajulugaru liked Tirapati.

Muscular body, well-rounded shoulders, exercise … he was very fond of them.

Since Tirapati's body was chiselled like a black stone idol, as if molten steel was poured all over it, Somayajulu had great respect for him in spite of his caste.

He never left a class without saying, '*Tindi kaligina kanda galadoy / Kanda gala vadenu manishoy.*'*

As soon as he saw Tirapati, he welcomed him politely, found out why he had come and advised him, 'Okay, my son. You must make that bitch of a girl study till she gains the capacity to learn Bharatham and Ramayanam, without stopping her midway.'

After Tirapati said, 'Okay,' he sent Sorajjem to the class that taught the alphabet, 'a, aa,' and while bidding goodbye to Tirapati at the school compound, he said, 'Yera, what do you eat, steel pellets?' laughed, felt both the biceps of Tirapati, and said loudly twice, 'Very good, take good care of your body. Don't get into bad habits. What's left if the body is ruined? It's as if the entire life is ruined,' and let him go.

Sorajjem's happiness knew no bounds. Excited with happiness, she sat in a corner.

In that class, children were like tiny tender leaves … like lily buds. If they opened their mouths, rows of teeth were like tiny little pomegranate seeds. Tiny little plaits, gowns of various colours, sweet little walk, steps, sounds …

The name of the teacher, provided by the government of independent India to teach them, was Sundarrao. Except in his name, there was not an iota of sweetness either in his walk, demeanour, looks or person. Everyone referred to him as Deaf Sundarrao. Except for that word, no other word was audible to him, no matter how much one shouted. He was completely deaf. Buck teeth – from his

* Lines from Gurajada Appa Rao's patriotic song which means 'With food come muscles / One with muscles is a man'.

mouth words came out as if stones were hurtling down mountains – a moustache as if bitten by lice, a crop of hair like the nest of a bottle-necked sparrow, a huge pot belly that moved away from his centre of gravity, a swagger-like walk as if he was playing chedugudu and as if he would fall on his face … he resembled a bear.

When one looked at him in that class, even for one without aesthetic taste or commonsense, he appeared like a porcupine in a jasmine yard.

In the beautiful dream Sorajjem would dream, Sundarrao was a rakshasa king.

His being deaf was indeed an injustice meted out by nature, but he would not agree. His belief was that his class children had ganged up and plotted to speak in such a manner that he could not hear. That was why he would beat the little kids one after the other hard with his cane for no reason at all.

Sorajjem did not know that teachers would beat children so badly. No sooner had she attended school for about a week, than she received blows till her body was terribly bruised.

Sundarrao would beat Sorajjem with a vengeance.

Annapoorna Sastri would come to this class now and then, and shout at Sundarrao about something. They were very good friends. Finally, just before leaving, he would take the cane from Sundarrao's hands, swing it in the air four or five times, feel happy at the 'juin … juin …' sound, finally use the last swing to beat Sorajjem and a couple of other Mala children, look at Sundarrao, give a loving smile, glare at the Mala children with his large eyes, and leave.

At that very tender age, Sorajjem realised that among people there were those that one ought to find distasteful.

Among the children at school, Mala children numbered less than ten. Though the other Mala children were almost Sorajjem's age, they were a bit brighter than her. Their fathers had an acre or half an acre of land and some belongings. Sorajjem was quite wretched. A feeling of inferiority that no one else had entered Sorajjem.

From the time the school started, the Chakalis would create a lot of noise. If the noise from the shore stopped by the afternoon, the rice mill right on that shore would start pounding. If it started with a '*chuk* … *chuk* …' it would continue yelling even after midnight.

During the rainy season water that leaked out of the thatched roofs did not appear like rain water but like dregs of discoloured brass, dirty, like water mixed with rubbish, and would fall in drops over the children. If those drops were to fall on the clothes, there was no way to remove the stain. If they rubbed hard to remove the stain, it would only grow much bigger.

Slowly, Sorajjem lost the joy of being in school and would now and again skip going. Whenever Tirapati came to know of it, he would warn her not to stop going to school. As days went by, Sorajjem was only thinking of ways to skip school.

Now, it looked as if Yenkadu had gone completely insane. His body had swollen like a corpse drowned in water. He would not say he was hungry … stringy beard … he would laugh and cry at the same time … would not go anywhere.

He would lie down curled or sit down crouched staring into nothingness, on a string cot in front of the hut.

Sorajjem was extremely fond of her father. Mother would go out to the fields and the hills to find food enough for each meal.

And Sorajjem had begun to stay at home to look after her father. Some time ago, Sundarrao had thrown her slate to the ground because she had not written 'ksha' properly. The slate was broken to pieces. She picked up the biggest of the pieces and carried it to school the next day. The children pounded that to pieces. The intolerance and vengeance the teachers showed on Sorajjem had passed on to the children. They too would tease Sorajjem. Using the excuse that she did not have a slate Sorajjem stopped going to school.

As her father was in a state where he could not attend to his own needs, she started to take care of him with utmost devotion.

One morning when she tried waking him up saying, 'Orey ayya, get up, it's late in the morning,' he did not get up.

Yenkadu had passed away. When he died, half the burden on his family had reduced.

IN THE RECENT past, the atmosphere around Mala Ramulori temple had changed. There were no '*Cheliyo chellako*' songs of the epics recited as in the past, but discussions about the atrocities of doras.

One day, Mala Sahadeva was beaten up by his boss, Yerra Satyamgaru. Sahadeva was neither a young person nor a weakling. He was over forty.

Yerra Satyam had come back in a rage, for some reason, from Gudivada, had asked Sahadeva, 'Have you fed the cattle?' and when Sahadeva answered, 'Not yet, dora,' he flung the choicest abuses at him, said, 'What were you doing all this while?' pounced on him and slapped him twice. Sahadevudu could have retaliated, but was stunned. In the meanwhile, Yerra Satyam's relative by marriage came from Kavataram. Sahadevudu wanted to preserve the prestige of his dora in the presence of the relative first and foremost, and so did not speak a word, came home from work, covered himself from head to toe and lay down.

Sahadevudu had joined Yerra Satyam's house as a chinna paleru when he was nine, became a pedda paleru, and toiled hard, doing all kinds of work for thirty years.

From carrying water to the house and herding the cattle, to tilling the land, planting the saplings, weeding, harvesting, gathering, husking and stacking in the granary, Sahadevudu did not do just one but all kinds of work for Yerra Satyam. How many days, how many years and how much work he had done! Continued to do so. For thirty years, he had handed over his body, his mind and all his energy to being a paleru of Yerra Satyam.

On returning home when his wife called out to him, as he lay completely covered under the sheet, 'What's it, mama?' he did not reply.

Even when the wretch of a daughter said, 'Olayya, look,' he did not respond.

Hearing his moans, through the torn black sheet, his wife, Koti bawled out crying, 'Orey, mama, what happened? Why has this come on us?'

Sitas, Ramas, Yenkatesus and Yakobus from the neighbouring huts gathered, 'What happened?'

'Nothing,' said Sahadevudu.

'Have you gone crazy then?' asked Chinnenkadu.

'Maybe he remembered his mother,' said Bucchi who worked for Achchigaru.

It had not been a month since Sahadevudu's mother had died of a serious illness, because of lack of medication.

All the people went back from where they came.

Koti asked Sahadevudu, who had not stopped crying, 'Mama, why are you crying so bitterly? What happened?' she kept asking him.

'Nothing. I don't feel good. Don't cry. I'll be all right in a while,' said Sahadevudu.

As her husband had shared at least something with her, Koti felt a bit calm.

Sahadevudu got up slowly and went to Ramulori temple. When he saw a number of people there, he could not contain himself and mumbled all the happenings to Pottenkadu who was sitting next to him. Pottenkadu told Shamelu.

'*Aa*, did he beat Sahadevudu?' All those who heard burned with fury, as if they had swallowed fire.

'It's okay if he had given a few blows when you were young. But how could he lay his hands on you now?' all of them said and surrounded him.

It's not as if Yerra Satyam had not beaten Sahadevudu some ten, fifteen years ago. Sahadevudu had not felt so bad then.

Shamelu said, 'Let's go immediately to the dora's house and ask, "What's this injustice? Aren't we human beings? Don't we have self-respect and prestige, modesty and honour?"'

'Don't ask just that! We need to take revenge. Sahadevudugadu must beat him up. We must all watch that,' said Tirapati.

Heated arguments and counter arguments took place. Each one felt ashamed as if Yerra Satyam had beaten them.

They shouted impatiently. Frenzied anger and thoughts commingled and finally they decided to go to Yerra Satyam's place immediately.

Tirapati got up saying, 'Now, let's go!'

'Let's go, but what are we going to say?' some said, not getting up.

'Let's decide on that after going there, first get up!'

'If that's so, that's the end. Each one will be pulling in different directions. Yerra Satyam is too clever for words,' said Kotesu.

'That too is true ...' a couple of them joined in.

Then, they debated both sides, exchanged views, and said, 'Let's nod our heads to all that Tirapati says,' and set out.

All along the way, they talked only about Sahadevudu's good qualities. They were furious at this extreme act of having beaten Sahadevudu, who had toiled doing all kinds of dirty work for thirty years, without even an iota of consideration. Sahadevudu was a soft person and would not speak even a word unnecessarily. He was like a cow that would not aim its horns at anyone.

Sahadevudu and some other coolies had been toiling hard to increase the yield in Yerra Satyam's fields year after year. They had changed the look of his house. In the place of a tiled house, there rose a house with a terrace and high walls all around. Yerra Satyam performed the wedding ceremonies of his children in a grand manner in this house.

The look of the cattle shed had changed. The thatched shed turned into a tiled shed. Buffaloes, cows and bullocks had grown in number. Their comforts too had grown.

Yerra Satyam had got used to a life of pleasure in Gudivada, and his coming to the village had become very rare.

Whether Yerra Satyam was in the village or not, Sahadevudu would work without making a single mistake in the fields. His goodness, his selflessness, his nature of working wholeheartedly, his blind faith in his dora – the result was this!

Mala men came on to the streets and were walking under a heavily clouded sky, before a downpour, towards Yerra Satyam's house.

Having forgotten that he had thrashed a paleru in the evening, not wanting to remember it, Yerra Satyam was sleeping without a worry on a high cot covered with a mosquito net on the terrace to which rooms had been added all around. There was no chance of his knowing that in a little while from then, at eleven at night, Malapalli would descend on him … till it came and descended on him …

The anger, disgust and contempt that Sahadevudu felt for his dora that evening was abating little by little as he walked along with everyone. He wondered, 'Looking at their manner, it appears as if they'll slice the dora at one go.' When he thought so, he was drenched in sweat in that rainy wind.

The respect for his master that flowed through every vein in his body made Sahadevudu fearful of what would happen.

He told Kantigadu who was next to him, 'Shall we let him go this time?'

'If you say that once again, I'll stab you instead of him,' Kantigadu replied.

There was a huge compound wall around Yerra Satyam's terraced house. That wall had high doors. They were bolted from inside. Now Yerra Satyam was a king within a fort!

After everyone assembled before the doors, they felt a little constrained.

'After getting there we should do this first. After that we should do in this manner. Such and such a person should say such and such a thing. If he behaves in that manner, we should behave in this manner' – none of this had been discussed earlier, so standing there in that manner felt strange.

That's why the compound around the house and the doors that had been there for five years suddenly came as an obstruction to all of them.

Everyone turned to Sahadevudu and said, 'Call him out.'

He hesitated a bit, knocked lightly on the door and shouted loudly, 'Dora!' Words would not come out of his mouth.

The dora did not get up, but the dorasani was still awake. She heard Sahadevudu shout, and came and opened the door.

The minute she opened, she was frightened on seeing the Mala mob. She could not imagine why this came to be, as she had no clue that the dora had thrashed Sahadevudu that evening. She only knew that he had beaten her.

That evening, when she was making buttermilk with a churner, she had thought, 'Why this wretched life? I work so hard. I've given birth to so many children. Have got them married. Despite growing old, he hasn't stopped running after prostitutes in Gudivada. In fact, it is there that he leads a family life. Moreover, whenever he comes home, he beats me up. It's good only when he goes out and goes behind prostitutes and wretched fellows, and doesn't come home. Wretched fellow!'

'Why has the entire Mala mob descended on the house at midnight?' she thought. She expressed the same feelings, 'What's it, Sadevudu? Why all these fellows … why have they come?'

'That's what we have come to find out. Call that fellow,' said Tirapati.

'Who?'

'That fellow, the dora.'

'*Aa* …' She had never imagined in her life that a Mala son of a whore would address her husband, heir to a huge sum of wealth, an older person, a respectable person and much more, as 'that fellow'.

She was shocked yet again.

At the screams, 'Call him … call,' she ran inside.

She went near her husband's cot and said in a feeble voice, 'Here, please …'

'What's it? Is it morning already?'

'That's not it … all of them have come,' she said, scared.

'Who, why the hell don't you say properly?'

'All the Malas have come. For some reason, I am terrified.'

'All the Malas? Has Sahadevudugadu also come?'

'Yes, he's right in front. He's standing like a dumb fellow. Doesn't say a word.'

'Oh, that's the thing is it? So it has come to this. Okay, I'll see!' Yerra Satyam said, and got up in a rage.

'Careful! Don't get into a fight with them.'

'Fight? You cowardly bitch … Won't I bury each one of them? Just because I beat the paleru once, will they attack me?' Yerra Satyam said, adjusting his pancha, and went in a rage to the entrance facing the street.

They appeared to be not less than twenty. Beneath the raised platforms, beneath the steps.

Dora climbed on to the raised platform.

'What's this, you sons of whores? Is it morning for all your quarrels? Why have you come rushing to my house all together? Have I slept with your wives? … Why doesn't even one of you speak?' Yerra Satyam was swaying with arrogance.

Two or three doras, who had got up feeling there was some commotion in front of Yerra Satyam's house, came there.

A person who had got up hearing the dogs bark, seeing so many people gathered there, turned back and ran to inform a few others.

'You fellow, Sadeva? What happened? Why have all these people come?'

'You thrashed me in the evening, didn't you? That's why they have come … to ask you, dora.'

'Dora? If you still remember I am the dora, would you have behaved like this? You demonic sons of whores. Even as you kill, you'll say, "We're killing you." What will they ask me? Let them ask me. Will they ask me if I have beaten you? I have beaten him! I have beaten him, not just him, beaten my younger son too, and beaten my wife too. Ask me. Ask me why I have beaten them too. Just like my son, just like my wife, this Sadevudu too is just the same. I will feed them when I have to feed them. I will beat them when I have to beat them. If I don't beat them, who else will beat them? I alone will beat them, I alone will kill them. When I feed them, don't I have the right to beat them?'

'Are you feeding him for nothing?' said Tirapati angrily.

'You are saying you are doling out to him, doling out. Are you doling out, out of kindness dora?' said Shamelu.

Four or five Malas said the same thing in four or five different ways.

'When he is toiling hard day and night, slaving for you, you throw a few grains at him. That's all, isn't it? He's not rolling on silk mattresses, he's not eating exotic food. He's sleeping on a hard floor. He's drinking a bit of gruel. He's working hard and earning for you. As if that's not enough, you have hit a man who has a son grown enough to marry. You must admit your mistake and ask forgiveness of our Sadevudu,' said Tirapati throwing back his head.

When Tirapati said this, Yerra Satyam felt bad, as if his entire prestige had been drowned in the Ganga.

'Orey, Tirapati, aren't you Yerrenkadu's son? You too have gone *yerri**, you crazy son of a whore. Not only have you gone crazy, you have made the Mala sons of whores too crazy, and have come to

* There is a pun here on part of the name of Yerrenkadu where 'yerri' means crazy.

wage a war with me at midnight. All of you have only Mala brains! You are the kind who would not hesitate even to thrash the breasts of your mothers. Now get off from my sight, won't you?' he said, and started to use abusive language.

His natural caste arrogance, arrogance of status and arrogance of wealth were making him burst out in this manner.

Three or four elders assembled asking, 'What's it, what happened?'

Mala people's blood was boiling at Yerra Satyam's words.

'Stop this string of abuses and tell Sadevudu you have committed a mistake, that your mind was not in its proper place,' said Tirapati.

Yerra Satyam* reddened all the more.

'Arey, Mala son of a whore. I won't rest till I see the end of you.' Saying this, he ran into the house as if to get a knife or an axe.

'Come, come, we have come here to see the end of you,' said Poligadu who had till then remained silent.

Everyone was highly incensed. But they did not know what was going to happen.

Then a few more doras arrived. Dorasanis too came and stood behind walls.

The old and the weary from Malapalli came.

The children ran and came. Paddalu, Sorajjem and Bodi too came.

Both sides were having heated discussions.

The threats of the upper-caste people and the protests of the lower caste people continued.

Brahmamgaru, who had earned the reputation of being a good and clever man, turned up.

All the Malas said, 'Salutations, dora.'

'Salutations. Why have you descended here at midnight? Do you think any time would do? Do you think there is no such thing as differences between the high and the low? You don't seem to realise that all of you coming together like this is a horrible crime. If you knew this, you wouldn't have come here. Now, at this very moment,

* There is a pun here on part of the name Yerra Satyam where 'yerra' means red.

you could all be thrown into jail since you have done such a thing. If they come to know that in a particular village, all the Mala people came and attacked the village, the government army from Delhi will come, kill you and perform the military drill, you crazy good-for-nothing people! You are naïve* and therefore are up to doing such crazy things. Otherwise, what kind of a man is Yerra Satyam – he never interferes with anyone, does not harm anyone. Are you showing your valour on such a person? In fact, he hardly lives in the village. Actually, when did he come into the village? Venkatraogaru, when did this man come into the village?' he asked Venkataiah.

Venkataiah forgot everything on being addressed respectfully as Venkatraogaru. That was why he was confused and could not respond.

'He came in the evening, dora,' said Sahadevudu.

Since the time Brahmamgaru arrived and tried to calm and scare the Mala people with his words, many of them listening to him had calmed down from weakness.

Poligadu said, 'That's not it, dora. You tell us what is just and unjust. You know, don't you, from when Sadevudu has been working and the kind of work he does? If he has thrashed him today, what should we make of it?'

'What? Did he beat him? *Che, che*! How could Satyamgaru do such a thing? I'll find out,' said Brahmam.

'Not find out. You must make him admit he has committed a crime and make him ask for forgiveness, right now, right here in front of all of us. Only then will we go back home,' said Tirapati.

'Make him admit it right away,' said Poligadu and Shamelu.

Brahmam was livid with anger. But he suppressed it and said outwardly, advocating for the doras, 'Tirapati, look at the words you used, "We won't go home till he asks for forgiveness." They are not in good taste. Tell me something, for I don't know, orey, Tirapati, isn't Satyamgaru like a father to Sadevudu? If Sadevudu makes him ask for forgiveness, will he be able to walk in the village tomorrow with his head held high? So, all of you forget these crazy thoughts

* The word 'yerri' is used here for both naïve and crazy. It is contrasted with anger denoted by 'yerra' in Yerra Satyam.

and go back home. I'll talk to Satyamgaru. If he beats Sadevudu one more time … not beat … even if he shouts at him a bit … come to me. That responsibility is on me …'

With those words, the elders of Malapalli around Brahmam said, 'Now, get going. Hasn't Bemmamgaru said that he'd take care of it if it happens one more time – now get moving! What has happened has happened. Now he'll see to it that it doesn't happen.'

Many youngsters too started slowly moving back.

Sahadevudu slid by Brahmam and went into the cattle shed. He went to look at the cattle and to ensure that the cattle had grass in front of them.

Tirapati, Poligadu, Shamelu, Kotesu and a couple of others too turned back to go home, unhappy and discontented.

KANNAIAH, ON HIS way back from Gudivada, said, 'Who's it that's going there?'

'It's me, Tirapati.'

'Why are you here at this hour …' and without giving Tirapati a chance to reply, said, 'How are your dora's fields? They say the fields are pest-ridden.'

'It has been controlled after we sprayed pesticide and put manure. They are green now.'

'How's the jute crop?'

'How can there be jute when the insects have licked it away?'

'The whole country seems to be in this wretched state. Is *thondangi** okay?'

'That too is over. Don't know what to feed the cattle from tomorrow.'

Kannaiah supported the stick on his neck, placed both his hands on the stick, said, 'I'll get going,' and left.

'You mother– … doras. All our lives are only to slave for them, isn't it? If their cattle have no fodder, what's it to us?' said Shamelu, who came just then and walked along with Tirapati.

---

* A type of grass fed to cattle.

'When I look at the cattle, I'm scared to death. All our lives … where will we work? Will our lives always be like this?'

~

SINCE THE SAHADEVUDU incident, the doras would fume with rage at Malapalli or Mala sons of whores. That did not mean that they had love for them earlier. Back then they neither had love nor rage.

They waited for the right opportunity … to break the bones of the sons of …

'No matter what. That Tirapatigadu … he will fold the entire village and eat it up. If we do him in, only then will the entire village be happy.' This was what the great men who protected the village firmly believed in.

That's why Nagabhushanamgaru would pick up a quarrel with Tirapati every now and again.

The minute Tirapati would come back from the southern fields, Nagabhushanam dora would ask, 'Orey, Tirapati, how's the water in the temple fields?'

'I've just come back from the southern fields. There's enough water. I've shut the outlets and come back. I'll go there after I've had my food.'

'It seems you were in a hurry to shut the outlets. There's no one to tend temple fields. Go after the saplings have dried and died. Orey, Tirapatiga, if you want to work, do it, otherwise bid me goodbye and say, "Ayya, Nagabhushanamgaru, namaskaram. I'm leaving. I'm giving up the work of a paleru under you. I can live just by politicking." If you want to go, I will myself bid you goodbye.' Nagabhushanam had been raving in this manner quite often of late.

But in reality, it would be a big loss if Tirapati were to leave his work as a paleru.

Tirapati worked extremely hard. Even if he employed three people they could not slave as much as Tirapati.

But the big people of the village would accost him and say, 'What's this, bava? That fellow, that Tirapatigadu is like that. *Ooo*, look after him, look after him, look after him well. It's like feeding a snake with milk, and I believe there was once a man just like you.

'One day he will wield the stick at you. Then you'll know. You'll think "I didn't listen to all our people when they told me so. What shall I do now?" At that time none of us will be in a position to help you.

'Listen to me. Remove him under some pretext or the other. It's true, he does a lot of work. If he goes you won't get another person like him. That too is true. But … All days are not ours. We must be very careful with people like him. None of our people will employ him. I'll give it to you in writing. Remember that.' There were many brothers-in-law, paternal uncles and maternal uncles, filling the market place, warning Nagabhushanam in this manner whenever he went out.

Not just because they told him, Nagabhushanam was also very angry that Tirapatigadu had led the people who had gone to beat up Yerra Satyam.

Nagabhushanam found it all the more distasteful to see Tirapati unmoved when he said, 'Go, go and become a leader.'

He would not say, 'That's not it, dora. Foolishness of a young fellow. It was a mistake that day, done knowingly or unknowingly.'

Moreover, Tirapati said once, 'I'm doing my work, dora, you're abusing me for no reason. If you think you don't need me, you may remove me from work. I will not stop working on my own.'

That was why Nagabhushanam blamed Tirapati for the death of a precious bullock tied on the right side of the yoke and said, 'Don't come to work from tomorrow.'

Tirapati was extremely fond of that bullock. Even at that moment of deep sorrow, he was enraged at Nagabhushanam's words.

Had it been some other day, he would have said, 'Why are you removing me from work?'

Or he might have said, 'Give me what is due to me till full moon day,' or wonder what else he would have done, but he stopped coming from the very next day without uttering a word.

When Paddalu came to know he had given up work as paleru, she said, 'God, what can we do? Will we get coolie work every day, God? From now on you are the sole protector of this coolie home,' and slapped herself, and threw a namaskaram to the wind.

When Paddalu lowered her eyes from the roof of the hut, they fell on Sorajjem.

Sorajjem could do all the work at home now.

'What if we put her to work somewhere?' thought Paddalu.

THE PRICE OF paddy shot up. The price of rice shot up. The price of pulses shot up. Along with this the price of land shot up exorbitantly. Not just in Malapalli but also in Kammapeta and Salipeta, the number of crumbling huts grew. Poverty increased. Diseases increased. Destitute deaths increased. Woeful cries increased. What did not increase? Everything increased. Except coolie rates. Again it was time to plant saplings. Discussions began at the Mala Ramulori temple.

Now Tirapati had turned into a coolie. A daily-wage labourer. Feast when he found work, starve when he didn't.

When they went to Komati Rosaiah's house for something, the Komati would give half of what he used to give for the same amount. If they said, 'What Komatayana, how unfair?' he would say, 'What can I do, things are so scorching high in Gudivada?'

If they said, 'Why don't you haggle in Gudivada?' Rosaiah would say, 'They say, it's scorching in Bezavada.' Whether it scorched anywhere or not, the coolie people's stomachs were scorching for sure!

If one were to look at the fields, they were yielding good crops.

What was all this then?

That was why all the coolies and such had assembled near Mala Ramulori temple.

Among the coolies, there were not only Malas, but also all the poor people of the village.

There were Salis, Mangalis, Chakalis, Kummaris* and Kunkapus† among them. During normal days, all of these people were into their own caste occupations.

---

* Kummaris are potters.

† People of a particular caste who sell kumkum, different kinds of beads, safety pins, etc.

In the recent past it had become common for people from other castes too to come for sowing, reaping and gathering. What else could they do? No other occupation could feed them properly. Finally, there were also a few poor farmers.

The two or three acres they had would not be enough for their families, even for their smallest needs. Almost every family had loans to repay, handed down generations … weddings of girls, litigations, all kinds of problems continued to exist. So, though a farmer in name, he had no choice but to go for coolie work.

This time, all the coolies in the village decided, 'We must raise our coolie rates. If all of us stand united, the rate is sure to increase.'

There was a chronic doubter. He said, 'Orey, keep quiet. Don't make a hue and cry. Just because we say we won't plant the saplings, will the village keep quiet? Loads and loads of people will descend from the neighbouring villages. "C" … for a crore of people. Some old woman thinks that if her cock doesn't crow, the dawn won't break.'

'That's enough, enough, you ill-omened bird of a wretched fellow! No one will come from another village. Don't they have to plant saplings too? Are they dying because they can't find coolie work? If we let go of this opportunity, there won't be another one. Do you think this is some weeding job? It's planting. If you delay, won't the saplings accumulate and become useless? Even so, if people come, we'll tell them. No one will come. Aren't they too human beings? Will they burn our stomach and eat bloody food?

'In fact, they too would want the coolie rates to increase. If it comes to that, we'll talk to the coolies in the villages around us – That we should ask for a hike in the rates like this. People will listen to us in Siddhantam, in Dentukuru, in Palaparru and in Koduru. There are many of our people there. How will even they survive working for this coolie rate?' Tirapati spoke of his plan in a forceful manner.

Everyone was happy about the plan.

'That's in fact true. If the time for planting the saplings is over, there would be no point no matter how much the coolies argue. The coolie rates will not increase a bit. For transplanting, each one would want the saplings to be planted first and so they will have to raise the rate. It's not such a burden on the doras too. The price of paddy has gone up. The price of land too has increased. So, during harvesting, if they increase the coolie rate by half a rupee, they won't suffer a loss. But if we ask them normally, they won't agree. They can't refuse if all of us are together.'

They thought of everything. All of them decided to be united. All of them decided firmly to be united and have their coolie rates hiked.

As always, the rich landlord, Purushottamarao sent word to Pottenkadu, 'All of you come to the eastern fields early tomorrow morning.'

Doras heard people talk – 'Coolie sons of ... want their coolie rates hiked. Pottenkadu has taken Tirapati and a couple of others and gone to the dora.'

'I'll come wherever you want me to, whenever you want me to, but ...' Pottenkadu stopped.

'What do you mean by but ... or half an anna*...'

'It's not something you don't know. We are poor sons of wretches. We are unable to have even gruel. You must increase our wages this time, dora; please increase them by half a rupee. That's enough. We won't ask you to increase a lot all of a sudden. Half a rupee for every person, that's enough.'

'Are you saying that's enough? How can half be enough? We'll increase it by two rupees. You can have it.'

'Don't say that, dora! It's not as if you are unaware of the times. We're poor people. If you increase, the others too will increase. All our lives are in your hands, dora.'

'Yes. It's not just your lives that are in my hands. Even the lives of small peasants. I don't care, I'll increase your wage. But all the peasants will attack me that I have ruined their lives. Even so, you keep grumbling ... but what does a man who does agriculture get today, nothing. There's nothing as useless as agriculture. You coolie sons of wretches are better off. You are able to see at least some money.'

---

* There is a play on the word kanee, i.e. 'but', that appears in the previous sentence. Kanee denotes both 'but' and the currency.

'Don't say that, dora.'

'Arey, don't make a hue and cry. I'll increase by a *beda*[*] per person. Don't argue, be in the fields tomorrow by seven. I'm getting the saplings pulled out. By then our people would have got down to the fields.'

'Okay, we'll be at the fields by seven, but increase our wages by half, dora.'

'What's it ra, don't you want to listen to what the person on this side is saying?'

'Please, you too listen to what we're saying. We too are human beings,' said Tirapati.

'What, are you threatening me?'

Pottenkadu said, 'No, dora. Who are we and what are our lives, are we the kind to threaten?'

'Arey, all that's unnecessary. I'll increase it by a beda per person. Come if you want to, or … tell me so, I'll take care of my problems. Don't you dare think that the fields will be left fallow just because you say you won't come? In a year you get coolie work for three months. Don't you kick even that and starve your family and children. Don't you become arrogant and invite all kinds of problems.'

'Rather than live a living death, half fed, it's better to die. But dora, we'll live praising you, we've children. We won't forget your benevolence.'

'Orey, the good I've done so far, your recognising it – enough of all that, I'll increase by a beda. Tell me once and for all if you're coming or not.'

'If you increase it by half, we'll come, dora.'

'Arrogant son of a whore, I'll increase it by a beda, will you come or not?'

'We won't, dora.'

'Okay, get going. If you step on my threshold again, I'll kill each one of you sons of … If you come to me again asking for this or that, then I'll show you who I am, now this is the end. If you ask for half, I have to increase by half, if you say increase by two, I must increase by two. Rather than that, it's better for us to hold a begging bowl, sell

[*] *Beda* is one-eighth of a rupee.

our lands and all, and leave. Rather than have you plant saplings, I'll let my fields lie like that, I'll not increase your wage by even a kanee. Let me see what you do.' Purushottamarao was incensed as if injustice was done to him.

Wasn't it unjust for the coolies to raise their horns and oppose him now, for from the time of their grandfathers and fathers, they had only nodded yes to whatever was said.

As the coolies were turning back, the dora raised his head to see, like a snake spreading its hood.

Though only four had stepped on to his threshold, the moment they stepped out, thirty people surrounded them.

'Oho! They are indeed united! Let them be ...' the dora felt, turned his head, spat out from the front yard, and went in.

All the coolies were chatting with Tirapati and walking along. All of them were going together. They tied towels round their heads. Their clothes were in tatters. Faded panchas. Banians that seemed to have been cut off till the armpits. As they were not well-built, they looked tall.

'Now what'll happen?' asked Chakali Guravaiah.

'What'll happen? Nothing will happen. He'll send word in the evening. He'll say he'll increase by four annas and ask us to come. We'll say we won't come. Again he'll shout a few abuses,' said Tirapati nonchalantly.

All of them burst out laughing happily.

'NARSAIAH, RAMULU, WHERE the hell are you? You mother– ... come here quickly.' By then, the two, and along with them the chinna paleru, Nagesu, and the servant girl, Lachi, all had come running and stood respectfully in front of Purushottamaraogaru.

'What should we do now ... I thought those sons of whores would yield to a raise of a beda or a *pavala*, I had all the leaves removed. They are riding a high horse. Don't we have anyone else other than them to depend on? There's no time to get people from the Nizam or from the west. Every year it was not possible for them to go to other people's fields, till the planting in our fields were over. Now, it has come to this.'

'What's happened even now? When you don't raise, why will the others raise? If it has to be raised you have to do it first, and our fields must be the first to have saplings planted.'

'I said I won't raise more than a beda even if my life were at stake. We must start work tomorrow itself, as if to insult them.'

'We'll go to Yelpuru and fix the coolies,' said Narsaiah and Ramulu, the loyal servants.

'Okay, get going. You should be back in no time. The coolies must get into the fields early tomorrow morning,' Purushottamarao said, twirling his moustache.

As Ramulu and Narsaiah crossed Salipeta and climbed on to the canal bund, Mangali Janaki Ramudu came upon them and asked, smiling a little and rotating his eyeballs, 'Up to where are you going? You've set out in the evening.'

'We're going to Yelpuru. All our people are protesting, right? Our dora has asked us to talk to the people from there for the planting of saplings, and bring them over by the night. That's why we're going.' The two of them left taking long steps.

As Mangali Janaggadu was going the same way after crossing his house, his five-year-old daughter followed him shouting, 'Nanna, nanna, nannay.'

'You mother– ... go back home. When I'm going on important *work*, wretched nagging!' he tried to threaten her, and walked briskly towards Malapalli.

After whispering into Tirapati's ears that Purushottamarao's people had gone to Yelpuru, he returned to the village.

That Mangali Janaki Ramudu gave this very important information to Tirapati was not due to the compassion he had for poor people like him. Not because he was pained that the doras were being unjust to the coolies. This was his habit. If he set out to shave and give a haircut, he could not resist from passing on the happenings in one house to the other. What he would hear in the first house, he would tell in the second house. He would tell the third house what he heard in the second house along with what he had heard in the first. He would tell the fourth house, everything that he had heard in the third house along with what he had heard in the second and first houses. The waves of news would go on endlessly.

So, only out of habit, he conveyed the information to Tirapati.

The poorer peasants sat on their haunches under the gangaravi tree and continued their conversation, 'How is Purushottamarao going to have the saplings planted tomorrow? He has had the saplings plucked and tied into bundles. They will rot if they are not used up within two days,' said Nageswarrao.

Lakshmaiah waited a bit and said, 'By now the coolies would have crossed Yelpuru's outskirts.'

'How come? Will they find people so quickly? They too have started planting, haven't they?' said Chalapati.

'Where have they started? Where have they started – who told you that? They won't start planting saplings there for four more days. The canals aren't ready. The fields too are not yet damp. I've just returned from there … I've admitted my younger daughter for training in Bandar, right? I put her on the bus at Angaluru and came through Siddhantam road. In fact, even the levelling of the field after furrowing hasn't been done so far,' said Lakshmaiah.

'So what about us, baba? Purushottamaraogaru can put up with a rupee this way or that. What about people like us if they say we won't come unless you increase our coolie?' Rangaiah said, frightened.

Lakshmaiah replied, 'Orere, Rangaiahbabu. Shall I tell you a secret? When I went to the western lake with pots to bring water, I saw Purushottamarao who said, "O, Lakshmaiah mama, this year the coolies are asking for a hike. Poor things, they've got to live, no? I can increase but the poorer peasants will attack me, I thought. When I said, okay, I'll increase without forcing others, they said an emphatic no. So, I won't increase and won't be abused by all of them. I'll give up my life but I won't break my word. All of you too don't call the people of our village. If not today, they will come down their high horse tomorrow."

'Then Veeraiahannayya, do you mean to say that Purushottamaraogaru didn't increase the rate just because of us?' Kannaiah asked, as he inhaled in the *chutta** smoke.

---

* *Chutta* is a country cigar.

'Orey, Kesavulu. Listen, I'll tell you a secret. How many acres do you have, how many do I have, how many does Rangadu have, how many does Chalapati have? Even if we add up our fields together, it won't be half as much as Purushottamarao's fields. If I increase the coolie, how much cost do you think I'll incur? If you put it at five per acre, it'll be five times five … how much is five times five? … wait, I'll tell you … five and five ten and fifteen … twenty-five … five times five, for twenty-five people, it'll be twenty-five halves, that is twelve-and-a-half. How much have I increased? For that reason, if I plant a few days later … if it rains on the day I plant, planting again … that'll be the end of me. My agriculture will be like the Bembadu's agriculture. The big people will always say such things. It's not for us alone that he hasn't hiked the coolie wages. It would cost a thousand or more for his hundred acres. That's why he's refusing to hike the coolie wages. Even if he gets coolies from Yelpuru, it's only to threaten them. How's it possible for them to do the entire job?' As he poured out the entire essence of his experience in the form of secrets, Lakshmaiah, who was stretching his body, threw the chutta in the stream in front of him and saw Janaki Ramudu come that way.

'Orey, you mother– … Janagga, may I burn you alive! No matter how many times I say, you don't learn. Doesn't our Chakali Ravudu have it? What … a donkey, the donkey there and you here … What's it, that wretched laugh and you. I'm just coming back after putting my daughter on the bus. I sent word to you early in the morning through Baligadu and you said you were coming just then. I have had to have this wretched beard and go about many villages. They won't blame me they'll only blame you, Janagga. What kind of a Mangali is he, he seems such a lazy fellow, they'll think. Orey, Janagga, shall I tell you a secret? …' Lakshmaiah went on.

'What can you say, Lakshmaiahgaru, I'll tell you. You know our Tirapatigadu. He and four or five others are going together to Yelpuru. Haven't our Purushottamaraogaru's people gone to Yelpuru, saying they want to get coolies? These people are also going there … to ask them not to come … if that happens … there'll be a lot of commotion.' Janaki was extremely excited that he alone was able to convey those things.

Even after having said this, Janaki Ramudu's excitement did not abate. His mind would not rest till he went to Purushottamarao's house and gave this information.

AFTER GIVING AN advance in Yelpuru saying, 'We'll get into the fields by seven tomorrow morning,' and having sought assurance from the headman, Narsaiah and Ramulu were on their way back when they saw Tirapati and five others coming in their direction, felt their heart in their mouth, and reached the village running through lanes and by-lanes.

Tirapati and the others met the coolies in Yelpuru and explained everything in detail.

'Is that what happened … those wretched rogues said all kinds of things, "There aren't enough people. Everyone has started planting at the same time." We thought all that was true,' said the headman.

'That's not it, annaya. These doras are the kind to create trouble between people like us and enjoy the benefits. You also go on strike that you want an increase of at least half. Since we are on strike, you should not come even if they hike the coolie wages. If you go on strike, will we come? We'll go right now and inform people at Dentukuru and Siddhantam. Someone from among you, please go and tell those at Angaluru. All prices are soaring high. When we're asking for just half, they're refusing us. We'll see how the work will proceed.' The headman was happy to see Tirapati talking with such vehemence.

The headman patted Tirapati on his shoulders and said appreciatively, 'Well done, bidda. Just one person like you in every village – that's enough … Go ahead. If need be, we'll meet again.'

Tirapati and his friends were returning, happy that things had happened more easily than anticipated.

'Arey, Yenkanna, you go to Dentukuru and inform your bava and others, and come back. If you wish to, take Rattigadu along … Rattiga, will you go?' asked Tirapati.

'Don't say will you go, say "Go" – that's it. We'll say yes to whatever you say,' Ratti said quite vociferously.

When they reached the drain canal, the two of them set out on the road to Dentukuru.

Just before dawn, amidst the screeching of crickets –

In the rumbling sounds of the field and drain canals running side by side –

In the dense darkness of dark clouds where even the twinkle of stars was not visible –

In the darkness where one could not spot the other –

Tirapati and his two followers were walking – sloshing on slush, slipping, falling, getting up –

After reaching the sluice-gates –

Without their having the opportunity to notice five shapes emerge from next to the dilapidated well, from behind the palm tree, and surround them –

'Amma,' Tirapati's loud scream,

'Amma,' from Chandrigadu too,

'Amma,' from Poligadu too.

A huge lightning of their heart-rending cries, 'Ammo, ammo' lit that darkness.

Birds that were trembling, waiting for the rain to fall, heard those horrendous shrieks, cried, '*ker, ker,*' and flew away in the darkness, flapping their wings.

Chandrigadu and Poligadu fell into the field next to where they stood.

Tirapati fell into the full, intense and fast-flowing waters at the sluice-gate.

The five shapes that had taken their lives vanished fearing their lives, carrying in their hands the knives that took the lives.

IT DAWNED.

The two who had gone to Dentukuru returned home and were looking out for Tirapati so they could tell him that their task had been successfully accomplished.

As Tirapati and others had not come back at night, all the Malas and coolies rushed to Yelpuru.

They saw Chandrigadu and Poligadu dead in pools of blood.

On the third day they found Tirapati's dead body near the tenth milestone just below the canal. In a state where even identification was very difficult.

Police and courts extracted a lot of evidence.

The police cooked up a new story and informed the villagers that when the coolies went on strike asking for a hike in wages, there were heated arguments within that led to murder, and put Yenkanna and Rattigadu in jail.

Purushottamarao had houses built for the sub-inspector and circle inspector in Gudivada Pati locality.

Everyone knew who had killed Tirapati, Chandrigadu and Poligadu, and who put Yenkanna and Rattigadu in jail.

But –

The police were in Purushottamarao's hands.

The courts too were in Purushottamarao's backyard.

Law and justice were caught in the smile of the bushy moustache of Purushottamarao.

Revenge burned in the hearts of every coolie. But, no one knew what to do and how to cool that anger.

For the present, Purushottamarao was getting work done by coolies of his own village without increasing even a beda, and was strutting about as if he had achieved something great.

AFTER HER SON'S death, Paddalu was afflicted by migraine.

To get rid of migraine, Mangali Ramudu squeezed a herbal extract into Paddalu's nostrils twice.

As he was squeezing the extract the second time, he said, 'As for the effect of this extract … that will have a great effect. By tomorrow you will have severe pain. But watch out for day-after. It'll vanish just like that. There won't even be a trace. Only if that happens, will you see me,' squeezed it and vanished just like that.

The headache tripled.

Sorajjem went looking for Ramudu for two days and brought him along.

'This time, try this extract. You haven't seen it. It's not like the other one,' he said, and squeezed a new extract.

Paddalu's skull felt an unbearable burning, her eyes dilated and she collapsed.

As Sorajjem began crying loudly a number of people gathered and the 'doctor' slipped out.

Paddalu opened her eyes after a part of the day had passed. And, Paddalu did not get off the bed after that.

She would place an alum bandage on her forehead, tie a cloth over it around her head, and keep groaning as she lay in a corner of the hut.

Brother's death, mother's bedridden illness – Sorajjem would always keep crying. Her sprightliness had completely disappeared. When she collected dung, when she collected twigs, she never uttered a word. She forgot what it was to laugh. Sometimes she would think that her brother would return home that day. Then she would remember that her brother was no more and would be overwhelmed with sorrow.

Since Sorajjem lost her sprightliness, Bodi too lost her sprightliness. Both of them would sit silently in front of the hut like mad people.

Paddalu and Sorajjem were unable to meet their food needs. Unable to meet their daily needs …

One day Paddalu gathered some energy and went to Anasuyamma's house.

Anasuyamma who was standing on the platform outside saw Paddalu come at a distance and went inside the house.

Paddalu came and shouted into the house, 'Anasuyammagoru … Anasuyammagorandi.'

'What's it? I'm coming.' Saying this, she sat next to the threshold.

There were five cots in the verandah. One cot was laid outside. Hens were flying and strutting about on it. In between they were spoiling it.

Next to it was a wooden easy-chair with its long arms stretched out. No one other than the head of the household sat on it.

No one had ever said no one could sit on it, but … no one would sit. Perhaps they did not say it because no one would sit –

There were three foldable chairs, five wooden planks and two mats in that house, but Anasuyamma never used any of them. Like many women she would sit on the floor next to the threshold or next to the chair or against the wall.

Anasuyamma, who now sat next to the threshold, said, 'What's it, Paddalu? You've come on some work. Poor wretched you, isn't it difficult for you to come at your age? Your son is no longer with you because of the wretched things he did.'

'Don't say such things, Anasuyammagoru. I'll salute you but my son did not do wretched things. Everyone knows that. That was his fate. This is my fate. What's the point in blaming anyone?' Paddalu said, and cried for a while.

'Keep quiet. Wretched thing, you must reconcile yourself for that's your fate. What are you doing? … you must have a wretch of a girl, right?'

'Yes, I have. If I didn't have her, I would have found a pit or a well, and left this wretched life. *Thallee*, what's there for me to live like this, like an anthill of diseases. She is a very young wretch. She has no elder sisters, no elder brothers, no father. Finally, if I too am not there for her, what will happen?'

'Osey! You wretched one, what's it? You are talking as if I won't rest if you don't die. Don't do such stupid things. The wretch of a girl won't be able to bear it.'

'That's why amma, I have hardened my heart and have been dragging this body along this way. Please employ her, dorasani.'

'What can that wretched chit of a girl do?'

When she heard those words, Paddalu was surprised even in her sorrowful state.

It was this same Anasuyamma who had repeatedly urged her, a year-and-a-half ago when Sorajjem was going to school, 'Send her to work, send her to work.'

When Paddalu had said at that time, 'The wretched young thing, what work can she do, dorasanamma?' she had said, 'What's her problem? If she could go to school, can't she work? Send her to me and I'll teach her everything. If she learns something, you'll get at least a few morsels of food. Why do you need education, you crazy wretched women? Will she take up a job?'

Now, after a year-and-a-half, here she was, saying, 'What can that wretched chit of a girl do?'

Paddalu wondered if what was inside Anasuyamma's mouth was a tongue or a piece of palm bark! But the need was Paddalu's.

If one were to ask whether Anasuyamma had no need for a servant girl … yes, her need too was great. She had been looking out for a servant girl. But now she only felt that if she were a little stern, she could reduce what she would have to pay them – that's all.

'Don't say that, amma! Sorajjem is over eleven. How can she still be a small girl? Aren't all the girls of her age going for coolie work? … Sorajjem has learnt to do things well, thallee, she'll do all that you ask her to do,' Paddalu pleaded.

Anasuyamma, pretending to think a bit, kept quiet and asked, 'Then, what do you want me to give?'

'Don't you know, ammagoru?'

'What do I know? I have been meaning to keep a wretched servant woman for the last ten years, but where did I keep one? Tell me, what do you want me to give?'

'Siti, Nagi's daughter, is just like her. She works in our Indiramma's house. They give her food twice a day, two sets of clothes a year and *pandum*[*].'

'Osi, you whore of a thief! What lies!'

'I won't say any more. It's left to you …'

'Okay … I can't spend so much. As for Indiramma, however much she spends, her husband will not say a word. It's not like that for me. I'll feed her and give her one set of clothes, good or bad. If that's okay, send her. And that too only because, you can't meet ends, and when you ask and I don't help my heart will torment me.'

'Okay, amma. Don't I know your heart? That's why I didn't go anywhere else and came directly to you. It's enough if she leads her life, thallee. I'll place her in your hands and I'll fend for myself, I'm a wretch of a woman who works. At least give her two sets and two sacks. We'll live, praising you,' said Paddalu meekly.

'Osey Paddalu, I didn't think you were such a stubborn wretched woman.'

'No, please don't think so.'

[*] Five sacks of grain.

'What is this then? No two bags, no nothing. I'll give two sets of clothes, but ... that too whatever I feel like giving ... later on don't say good ones, stupid ones, new ones, old ones ... don't talk anymore, just send her,' she said, and got up from next to the threshold.

'Okay, amma. I'm placing the girl in your hands. Please be a little kind to her, thallee. She is only a wretched child ... I'll send her from tomorrow onwards.'

'That's enough, all your parting messages. Will I eat her up? Why tomorrow, send her right away. Take her back after the sweeping in the evening is done.'

'All right, dorasanamma.'

As she returned home, Paddalu grew very worried, 'The girl has to slave day and night from now on.'

SORAJJEM WOULD GET up at dawn and go to Anasuyamma's house.

Anasuyamma's husband would be fast asleep.

Anasuyamma would be making buttermilk in the kitchen.

Sorajjem would take the broom and sweep the entire backyard clean.

After finishing that task, she would take the water from the bottom of the tub in a pot, go to the shed and bring dung, and would sprinkle dung water in the frontyard and in the backyard of the house.

It would just begin to become bright in the morning. Anasuyamma would surface with the muggu box in the verandah.

Now, the ritual of drawing a muggu on the ground would begin. Anasuyamma was extremely fond of drawing muggus. Without noticing anyone in front or behind her, not knowing how she looked or what she wore, she would be very involved in drawing muggus.

During that time, Sorajjem would sweep all the rooms.

She would keep the used vessels outside, and using husk, burnt pieces of dung, coconut fibre or a few straws of hay clumped together if she could not find the fibre, would scrub the vessels to a shine and then wash them.

After arranging the vessels she had washed, she would do one task or the other.

In the meanwhile, Anasuyamma would call out, 'Osey, Sorajjem. Go to the Komati's house …' and ask her to get something or the other.

As soon as she returned from the Komati's house, she would ask her to get something else saying, 'I forgot to tell you earlier …' and when she got that thing, she would ask, 'Did you get mustard?'

'You didn't ask for that.'

'If you lie, I'll kill you. I'm telling you now. Get going and get a kanee of mustard. You must come back this very minute.'

Sorajjem would run and get that too.

'You haven't washed half the utensils,' she would say pointing to the ones she had placed just then.

'All those weren't there when I washed, dorasani.'

'If they weren't there, what of that? They are there now … now clean them … clean them quickly, clean them quickly …' she would say and hurry her up.

After cleaning them and leaving them upturned in the kitchen, when she would just begin to think that the work was over for a bit, she would have to hold the younger dorasani by hand and leave her at school. All the children would go to school but Anasuyamma was scared.

'She's a young wretch. The school is on a bank of the lake. If she slips by mistake, imagine what'll happen … Don't let go of her hand as you take her and drop her off at school. After you come back, you can have your food.'

It would be after ten by the time she dropped the girl and returned. Anasuyamma would say, 'Okay, have your food, you wretch.' Then Sorajjem would get the *jaramasileri* (German silver) plate and glass that she had brought from her home and kept hidden in the roof of the cattle shed, and wait sitting near the threshold of the kitchen.

There was a small open drain that would flow out between the place Sorajjem would eat and the big tank. The hens would always be purposefully digging up the dirt. No matter how many times they were shooed away, they would go away only to return. All the time Sorajjem ate, the brood of hens would roam around her, taunt her and would leave only if she threw a morsel to one side.

Sorajjem would think that it would be wonderful to eat sitting in the verandah. Though Anasuyamma would see the hens taunting Sorajjem every day, she would never say, 'Sit and eat in the verandah.' She would keep quiet as if she knew nothing.

As she served her food, she would ask, 'Enough?' and Sorajjem would say, 'Umm.'

'You are a young bitch. Wouldn't you know if you're hungry or not? If you ask for more, you'll waste it. They say food is an incarnation of god. You shouldn't waste it. If this is not enough, ask for more.'

If she asked for more once in a while she would say, 'You wretched bitch. You are killing me, making me go this way and that. My legs are giving way, unable to move around. Can't you ask, once for all, all that you want?' On a day like this, of the food the dorasanamma served, Sorrajem would be able to get only that which was left after the hens had raided her plate.

After eating, she would wash her plate and glass, hide them in the roof of the cattle shed, wipe her mouth with her gown and wash the utensils again.

She would sweep the rooms again – hadn't the hens messed them up very badly?

She would drive the hens out of the house and into the cattle shed. While she returned after driving them away, the hens would be back again in the house and climb on to the cots much before Sorajjem came back. In a room in the house there was a large basket which was used to store paddy. The hens knew that if they pecked at the basket, a few grains would fall out. Eating a few grains, coming out scared that they'd be shooed away, and going back in again ...

Going into the kitchen, eating a few grains of rice ... if possible, the rice in the pot.

That is the way of the hens.

'It's going to be afternoon. Go, get the child from school.'

She would go to the school and get the child.

She would take her back to school again.

'Go to that one's house and get that.'

She would go to that one's house and get that.

'Go to this one's house and give this.'

She would go to this one's house, give this and return.

Everyone would have their lunch.

Again, she would keep cleaning utensils, and it would be evening by then.

She would do the evening sweeping, sprinkle dung water, wipe the lamps, clean the glass chimneys of the lamps with muggu, light the lamps … count all the hens and cover them under an upturned basket.

There would always be one hen lazing around even when darkness fell.

'I can't find the red-feathered hen, dorasani …'

'Search, search,' the dorasani would come out. Saying this, both of them would go round the backyard shouting, 'Bho, bho, bho, bho,' and asking those they met on the way.

After a while, the red-feathered hen would be seen near the hens' coop, 'Bho, bho.'

After counting all of them, covering them, after every one had eaten, after eating whatever Anasuyamma served her, after it was very dark, Sorajjem would set out towards her home.

IT MUST HAVE been two hours after dusk. Days before the new moon … even for those who could walk in darkness, this was pitch dark.

Sorajjem was walking hurriedly towards Malapalli, alone.

'Who's that?' a voice from the dark.

'It's me.'

'Me means who?' Chintadu asked from that darkness.

'What does it matter to you who I am?' said Sorajjem.

'Aha! Is that so? You're Sorajjem, aren't you?'

'Aha! Is that so? You're Sorajjem, aren't you?' Sorajjem imitated Chintadu. Chintadu was of the same age as Sorajjem.

'Osey, Sorajjem! I too am coming from that side, right? Why didn't you call me? We could have come together.'

'Orey, what hopes! If I have to come with someone, why should it be you?'

'Is it because I placed my leg and tripped you?'

'I didn't fall down.'

'Then why didn't you call me now? … We would have come together. You're alone … aren't you feeling afraid in this darkness?'

'What should I fear?'

'That's true, the devils themselves are scared of you.'

'The ghosts will shudder at your sight.'

Someone in front of them said from the darkness, 'Who's that?' Sorajjem replied like her mother, 'I am a Mala woman.'

'That's obvious,' said Chintadu from behind.

'Who's that fellow?' said the man in front from the darkness.

'I'm Chintadu.'

'Which Chintadu?'

'Chintadu of Betolla family.'

'Orey, is that you? They said Eerabaddarrao went to Gudivada. Has he returned?'

'Yes, he returned by dusk. Seems to be a bit better.'

'Okay, get going.' Saying this, the man in the dark gave permission to the two who had stepped away from his path.

'WHAT'S IT, YOUNG one!' said Veerabhadrarao seeing Sorajjem.

'My dorasanamma wanted me to ask Lalitammagoru and get a few bunches of curry leaves,' said Sorajjem.

'If your dorasanamma doesn't have a few bunches of curry leaves, would her curry not have a wonderful aroma?' Veerabhadrarao threw a charming comment at his neighbour, and said, 'Okay, go in and ask,' and shouted for Chintadu, 'Arey Chinta, my brother-in-law from Kavataram is coming, go and ask your father for fish.'

'My father just left for the drain canal.'

'If he goes there, will he get stuck there? Go quickly and tell him.

'Okay.'

'Don't just say okay and not go to him and get planted in your house. You have to feed the cattle. Not a single work has been done. You have to run and be back as if you haven't left the place, run.'

'Okay,' Chintadu said, and ran.

Chintadu was working as a chinna paleru at Veerabhadrarao's place. Though he was called a chinna paleru, there was no work that that chinna paleru did not do. On top of all this, dora's abuses. If it were only abuses, it would have been all right. Chintadu's father, Kotadu, would catch fish and eke out a livelihood selling fish.

From the time Kotadu had put Chintadu to work, he had to confront a new problem.

Every two or three days Veerabhadrarao would send word asking him to send fish. Kotadu would think, 'What does it matter who I give it to,' bring the fish and hand it over, the dora would take it and eat it but would not talk of money.

If he said, 'What dora …' he would shout into the house, 'Pour him some buttermilk,' or 'Give some pickle,' and shaking off the dust in the towel on his head, he would leave.

We must say things as they are – Lalitamma was a good person. So she was not the right person for Veerabhadrarao.

She would give some pickle, rice or buttermilk or both, but …

Kotadu did not like exchanging fish for pickle.

'Go ask doragaru and get some money … the fish you gave the other day had no thorns. They were very tasty. Ask ayyagaru and take money … bring those fish again,' she would say.

'Dora won't give, dorasani.'

Would he be able to find the dora to ask him?

That's why Chintadu did not like to give fish to Veerabhadrarao.

By the time Sorajjem had plucked the curry leaves and came out, she found Chintadu coming in gasping for breath.

He told Veerabhadrarao, who sat there rolling his chutta, 'My father came back home, but it seems he did not catch any fish.'

'Arey, Mala sons of whores, if you don't want to do something, you tell any number of lies. Tell your father I wish to talk to him urgently, and ask him to come,' he said and drove back Chintadu.

Chintadu and Sorajjem came out together.

'Yera, the fish really didn't fall in his net?' asked Sorajjem.

'Don't tell them, but …'

'My father said he'd go to Karimella. His basket is full of fish. He is going to sell them. "Your dora knows only to grab the fish but not to pay for them," he said angrily.'

'But what will you do now?' asked Sorajjem.

'I'll do something or the other, but don't tell even your dorasani …' Chintadu said, and ran towards Malapalli.

His mother said, 'Tell him he has taken the fishing line and gone to the canal, and that he would give the fish to him, if he catches any.

Chintadu sat at his place for two minutes and then returned to the dora's house.

'I believe my father took the fishing line and went to Jangalava canal, dora – my mother told me. If he catches any, he will bring them only to you,' said Chintadu.

'Do you think he will catch any?'

'I don't know. I believe the water is in full flow. It seems fish wouldn't be caught with a fishing line, but only with a spear.'

'Okay, what can we do? If your father gets them, fine. Otherwise get hold of that black hen. My brother-in-law is coming after a long time.' Saying this to Chintadu, he thought to himself, 'Moreover, I need his help with something else,' and went inside.

'No matter how many times he has given us fish, have you paid him a rupee even once? He ekes out a living selling fish. So how many times can he give you for free?' said Lalitamma.

'Osey, you mother– … Shut up. When you speak, you speak for the Mala sons of whores and Madiga sons of whores. What is this? Why this excess? Keeping a fellow incapable of tucking in his loin cloth, who the hell gives him four bagfuls by the end of a year – your father?' he jumped all over her.

'Okay … why bring my father in all this; as if you're giving four bagfuls for nothing – he's supposed to be young, but there is not a thing that he doesn't do. He works without making any excuses, and so you're giving him,' said Lalitamma.

'Osey, you mother– … you retort word for word! Your father spoilt you by educating you.'

'*Aa* … education … great education … I studied only till the fifth,' said Lalitamma.

'That's why you are taking out such law points. If you had studied a little further, you would have perhaps become a lawyer yourself!'

WHEN THE BEGINNING of the new farming season was a week away, Paddalu came to Anasuyamma.

'What's this Paddalu, you've shrunk like a black bead! Did you think that if you showed up I would eat you up?' said Anasuyamma.

'Did you need only me to eat up?' said Paddalu.

'Why have you come like this?'

'It's only that the new farming season is approaching, I came to talk about the chit of a girl ...'

'What's there to talk? Is she finding any problem in my house? I'm taking care of her better than my own child. Crazy bitch, she too has mingled in the house with us like one in the family,' said Anasuyamma. She thought to herself, no matter what, she should not say anything by mistake.

'... nothing dorasani ... wondered if you'd give a pandum this year ... came to ask you that ...' mumbled Paddalu.

Paddalu did not desire a pandum. Not that Anasuyamma would give a pandum either. She just thought, 'Let me broach the subject,' and proceeded to ask.

'Osey, you desire to rob like thieves! As if she has learnt all the work, you're asking for a pandum. If you don't like, take her away from here ... thallee, I can't keep her giving you a pandum of paddy.'

Though she was giving her food twice a day and two sets of clothes – she pretended that a pandum which was only five sacks meant fifty sacks, and that two meals and two sets of clothes cost her hundreds ... Anasuyamma went on and on.

Paddalu was perturbed and asked, 'What will you give then?'

'I won't give anything more. Ask her to work in the same way as before.'

'How can she do that, dorasani? Hasn't she grown up?'

'If she has grown up, won't she eat more food? Won't she need more cloth?'

'No, dorasani. Please tell me what you'll give.'

'I won't give even one bag.'

'You really won't?'

'No. I won't.'

'Farewell, dorasani. Then look out for another girl,' Paddalu said, and got up.

'Unless you, a Mala whore, asks me to look out for another girl, don't I know?' Paddalu and Anasuyamma broke off with each other. Paddalu took Sorajjem from one house to another.

She sent Sorajjem to work for Mahalakshmamma after ensuring that she would give her food twice a day, two sets of clothes and three bags of paddy.

Sorajjem began going to Mahalakshmamma's house to work.

Mahalakshmamma worked as a teacher. She was a straightforward person. No matter what she spoke, she spoke in a brusque manner. As soon as Sorajjem came, she made her sit and gave her a lecture.

'Osey, Sorajjem, I'll tell you what chores you have to do every day, listen. Don't irritate me, just do as I tell you,' she began to say.

'You must come as soon as there's light.

'As soon as you come you must sweep the front yard, the house and the backyard sparkling clean like a mirror.

'After you sweep, you must take out water from the bottom of the tub, mix dung in it and sprinkle dung water.

'After sprinkling the dung water, you must draw a four-part muggu.

'After the muggu, you must scrub the tub clean. Otherwise it will gather moss.

'After you scrub it, take a brass pitcher and go to the canal. Scrub and wash it clean. Bring water in that vessel and fill the tub.

'After the tub is filled, get water from the eastern lake for the large pot. Strain the water and fill the large pot. Ensure there's no dust or such. Then go get another pitcher of water – we can use it for drinking – keep it like that … you wretched thing … don't forget to cover it. Otherwise some insect or the other will cause diseases.

'Afterwards,

'You must wash all the utensils in the kitchen.

'You must light the stove.

'Light the fire pit.

'Put on the pot of horse gram.

'Then –

'You must take the buffalo to the canal bank. That's a good buffalo. It won't go anywhere away from the bank. You leave it there, come back and clean the entire cattle shed. Whenever you are free, eat *saddannam.** As per your wish. Eat as much as you want and as much as you can. There's no one who'll say no to you. The children and I will go to school.'

Sorajjem was not scared listening to the list of chores. Sorajjem felt great that she was working for a person who had a teaching job.

'Dorasanammagoru, what is your salary?' she asked enthusiastically.

'Why do you need all these details, do your work … Get the buffalo in the evening and tie it up. Put some grass for it. Every day put a jute bundle for it. After the horse gram has boiled, take it and keep it in a corner in the kitchen. Otherwise, dogs, hens or all kinds of animals will eat it up. You or I will have the horse gram water. Don't give this water to anyone else. That will have the entire essence of horse gram. If we give it to the buffalo, it will give us some milk at least. Can drink it happily. Osey … what's your name …'

'Sorajjem.'

'May my brain rot, osey, Sorajjem, I'll leave the entire house in your hands. Wonder how you'll look after it … *aa* … in the evening you must finish sweeping and milk the buffalo …'

'I don't know how, ammagoru.'

'Osey, you crazy-faced woman, you have grown up so much and say you can't milk a buffalo! You can learn it in two days. You can leave early after having your food … it's alright with me. It's enough if you're helpful to me a bit,' Mahalakshmamma said, indicating all that Sorajjem had to do, and made Sorajjem the 'queen' of the house from that day onwards.

Sorajjem found working in Mahalakshmamma's house easier than in Anasuyamma's though there was more work. Moreover, there was food to fill the stomach.

---

* The previous night's leftover rice eaten the following day as breakfast.

MAHALAKSHMAMMA HAD BEEN married young. Her husband, Kondalarao, worked as a clerk in Gudivada. Kondalarao was not useful either to his family or to himself.

Every month as soon as he got his salary, he would give up food and sleep and play cards day and night. Till the money got over.

After that he would give up on food and sleep, and go in search of money.

After that he would play cards again.

After that he would hunt again.

When the money in his hand would get over, his thumb would call out, 'Come, let's play cards, come let's play cards.'

His index finger would say, 'Where from can we get it and play, where from can we get it and play?'

His middle finger would say, 'Let's take a loan and play, let's take a loan and play.'

His ring finger would say, 'How will we repay the loan, how will we repay the loan?'

His little finger would say, 'Let's push it on the wife, let's push it on the wife.'

His brain and other organs would always think of playing cards and would be ecstatic.

'Babbabu, my life is at stake. Please give me a hundred,' he would tell anyone he met.

When the man would say, 'I don't have it,' he would say, 'Don't say that. If you say no, death is my only recourse. I am a man with kids. Don't ruin them.'

The man would feel bad, if he did not give money to Kondalarao he would perhaps be doing injustice to the children, and so he would put his hand into his pocket. In fact, Kondalarao would choose the person who would feel bad.

Okay, when he would notice that the person had softened, he would say, 'I'll write you a promissory note for two hundred and you can give me one hundred and twenty-five.'

That person would say, 'Why should I get your money wrongfully?' and write the note for the exact amount he would give.

Then the person would come after a few months asking, 'Where's my money?' wouldn't he?

'Money … where's the money? If I had money, why would I roam about the bazaars like this?' Kondalarao would joke.

The man who gave the money would cry hoarse, beating his head and mouth.

Then this man would feel sorry for him, 'Poor man, he gave a loan and feels deceived.'

Then, with a smile, he would say as if thinking far ahead, 'There's a way out. You do that,' he would say, 'First, give me ten rupees.'

After getting that ten, he would put it in his pocket, write Mahalakshmamma's name and address on a piece of paper immediately, and place the paper in his hand, as if he had paid off his debt.

'What's this? What do I do with this woman's address?' the creditor would say.

He would joke for a while saying, 'Scratch your tongue,' would laugh mockingly a few times, would hurt the heart of the man who gave him a loan, would rub chilli powder on the wound, and then say, 'You go straight to the woman in this address. She's my wife. Go to her, show her the note and say, "You repay the loan, or else I'll have your husband shoved into jail." If you ask her to repay the loan when she is in the school, the money will be in your hands the very same evening. The woman is very clever, but in front of prestige her cleverness comes to naught.'

The man who gave the loan would enthusiastically go and catch hold of Mahalakshmamma in school.

In Mahalakshmamma's opinion – 'No matter how horrible he may be, a husband is a husband after all.'

She would collect the money from the house – from the box, from here and there – and pay up the note.

Mahalakshmamma's husband would not come home that day or the next, but would come on the third day and put on a woebegone face, that he had borrowed from someone else, and lie down on the bed without eating and shed tears.

'Enough of crying now, get on with it,' Mahalakshmamma would say shoving food in front of him.

When she had been newly married, Mahalakshmamma would address her husband as 'Yevandi, Yevandi.' She would think that with her tact and patience she could change her husband. Very quickly she realised her strength. Finally, she got used to abuses, 'Dead man, fallen man,' and also to maintaining a card-playing husband.

NOTICING THAT SORAJJEM was doing her work neatly and responsibly, Mahalakshmamma was impressed. That's why when Sorajjem asked for something, she would not say she did not have it. She would not say no to her.

'Dorasanammagoru, so much of saddannam was left over.'

'I thought that that fallen fellow would come and so had some cooked. That fellow didn't turn up. Put it along with the cattle feed.'

'I'll keep it aside and take it for my mother.'

'Take it. Take that horse gram charu too … What does your mother eat? Whenever I see her she looks half dead.'

'What does she eat, stupid one? She doesn't eat anything.'

'If she doesn't eat, how will she live?'

'That's the thing! In Malapalli there are many like my mother. They drink a mouthful of gruel once every two or three mealtimes. That's it. If they could eat rice and curry for every meal, why would they be born in Malapalli?'

'Osey, curse be on you! Who taught you these words? If you are born a Mala, don't you have to eat?'

'How will they eat? If their birth is a Mala birth, where will they get food or happiness?'

'Osey, stupid woman! Everybody's birth is like that. Being born a Kamma, am I happy, haven't you been seeing?'

'What's there for you? You have a buffalo that gives two seers of milk. You have paddy fields. You have a majestic job. You have things on the stove. You have things under the stove. What is the similarity between you and us?'

'Osey, curse be on you! How much have you studied? I have everything but married life!'

'Don't say that! Doragoru is okay! He's like Dharmaraja*.'

* A character in the Mahabharata, eldest of the Pandavas.

'Yes, a Dharmaraja! You said the right thing! Those days that Dharmaraja may have made his wife cry and then died. If this fallen fellow dies, I'll mourn a bit and keep quiet. What's he achieving by living?' Mahalakshmamma controlled her tears and sent Sorajjem out saying, 'These woes are always there. Get up! Get up and go to the shop and get tamarind.'

As Sorajjem ran fast, she yelled out loud, called out to her and warned her, 'Osey! Don't say, "My dorasanamma abused her husband like this, and like that." It won't look good.'

'Why would I say? How can anyone not share their problems and happiness?' Sorajjem said, and took off.

She came back as quickly as she went, empty-handed –

'The Komati said that unless you settle at least part of your debt, he won't give anything on loan.'

'May he be cursed, why is he behaving in this wretched way? Does he think I'll run away from the village? That wretched fellow! Wasn't it less than a week ago that we paid him fifty rupees? I'll go and ask him why he can't give me, but get the bag, go ask Varalakshmamma and get some curds in a jiffy for setting, hasn't the cat overturned all the buttermilk … Whatever groceries one wants, aren't the husbands getting them from Gudivada? It'd be good if one did not buy even a matchbox from him. That'll serve him right. But which maharaja will get them for me from Gudivada … Osey, Yenkava,' she let out a loud scream seeing Chakali Yenkava walking on the street.

'What's it, amma?' Yenkava said, and came to the doorstep.

'When I sent the chit of a girl, he chased her away, but please go to the Komati's house, ask him to write a quarter seer of tamarind in my account and bring it.'

'Ayyo! I'm going to the Mangali's house. My old man is suffering from breathlessness. I thought I will get some medicine from the Mangali … I'll go get the tamarind in the evening.'

'What'll I do with it in the evening? Okay … Go. Does he have asthma?'

'Yes … He's literally jumping up and down. I'll take leave, ammagoru, please don't mistake me.'

As soon as Chakali Yenkava left, Malakshmamma set out with a bag.

Sorajjem took out the milk from the sling, kept it on the stove, took the cup and ran out to get the curds for setting. As Varalakshmamma's house had chamanti flowers, Sorajjem felt happy going to her place. If she asked her for a flower, she would give her.

Varalakshmamma made a horrid face when she saw the cup in Sorajjem's hands, 'Curse you! You touch even buttermilk, do you? Your dorasanamma is completely losing her mind.'

'Why, aren't we human beings?'

'*Aa* ... A human being. Can't you and your dorasanamma remember when you drink buttermilk that you must keep a bit of it for setting curds?'

'The cat spilt all of the buttermilk.'

'Where has your dorasanamma gone? There's not a sound anywhere. As if it has stopped raining.'

'She has gone to the Komati's house.'

'You seem to have gone there a little while ago?'

'He said he wouldn't give.'

'Wonder what the problem is ...' Saying this, she brought buttermilk in a cup. 'Next time, *you* don't come.'

After this Sorajjem did not feel like asking for a flower and was coming back quietly, Varalakshmamma said, 'Osey, Mala woman, pluck a flower.'

'No, thank you,' Sorajjem said angrily and went away.

SORAJJEM HAD STARTED wearing *paita* for a year now.*

It had been three years since she joined Mahalashmammagaru's house.

When Paddalu asked her to raise the salary, Mahalashmammagaru said an emphatic no.

'The girl has grown up. How come the same salary as three years ago?' said Paddalu.

* Wearing a *paita* indicates the girl having attained puberty.

'If she has grown up, won't she eat bigger mouthfuls? Am I asking her to do something new, for me to raise her salary?'

Paddalu requested her for a while and left. It was true that later, out of anger, Paddalu had burst out and said to another dorasani – "She repays the hundreds and thousands her husband takes as loans, but that thallee has no heart to increase even a sackful for a girl who slaves without respite!'

That talk promptly reached Mahalakshmamma.

She abused Paddulu badly in front of Sorajjem. 'I'll repay the loans my husband has taken! Should Mala whores advise me? Don't I know as much as a Mala woman? If there's someone who can give ten *puttis*[*] for the job she does, go and look for them.'

Sorajjem stopped going to work.

Mahalakshmamma sent word twice or thrice but Sorajjem absolutely refused to go.

AFTER THAT SHE was able to get to work at Yerra Suryamgaru's house.

Yerra Suryam was a farmer with twenty-five acres of land. He farmed it himself. Everything was looked after by palerus. They would be given food twice a day, two sets of clothes and a pandum of paddy. Reasonable pay.

It was there that Sankurattirigadu too joined as 'the young fellow only to tend cattle'. They gave him two meals a day and two bags of paddy.

Sankurattirigadu's work was to take the cows and buffaloes near the fields and along the bunds and bring them back. He had to push them into the canal, wash them, bring them home and give them the feed. If the dorasani, dora or the pedda paleru was milking the cow, he had to take the calf away and tie it up … such were his chores.

When he was free he would help Sorajjem.

From his childhood he had *love* for Sorajjem.

As for Sorajjem, she would always keep teasing him.

'When's the wedding of the young fellow tending the cattle?

'When all the cattle would enter the fields!'

[*] A large measure of paddy weighing approximately 250 kilograms.

She would sing thus and rile him.

Sankurattirigadu was just nine. Thin like dried palm coir, he would look like a six-year-old.

The cattle would never listen to him. All the time he tended the cattle, he would use the choicest of abuses.

'Osey! You mother–! … Wait, I'll have your horns chopped off. Chey, you … you tailless one! You don't have a tail, yet, you mother– … your pride hasn't vanished … chey … crooked-horned one … osey, get down, get down! Get down! If I come there …' Saying no, Sankurattirigadu abused all the cattle that had stepped into the canal and those that did not, one after the other, drove them from that side to this side and from this side to that side that evening.

But, none of the cattle listened to him, climbed on to the canal bund each in a different direction, got down into the field on the other side of the canal … that field belonged to Nallachantabbayigaru.

At that time the owner of the field was right there. Noticing the cattle coming into his field, he showered abuses, 'Orey! Who is that son of an ass who drove the cattle here, rey! Young son of a whore! How did you think you could control them when you drove them here to wash them, you Mala son of a whore! You mother– … you have ruined the entire field! As I was here at the right time, it has not become worse. You young son of a whore! Come here!' he took giant leaps, came, caught hold of Sankurattirigadu, twisted his ears, gave four or five blows on his head, and when he tried to run away he beat him badly on his back.

The young fellow burst out crying and ran this way and that.

'Son of a whore! If I see you again, I'll chop you to bits. Didn't you see your brother being tied and flogged. I'll do the same to you now,' the owner of the field abused him again and got down into his field.

Sankurattirigadu wanted to drive the cattle back home, and when they refused to listen to him, each of them running in a different direction, he threw the stick saying, 'You mother– … herd …' and started crying again.

In the meanwhile, the pedda paleru, Bandanaggadu came by and saw the situation.

From the other bund, the owner of the field yelled out loud to the pedda paleru:

'Bandanagga, is it you who sent this young son of a whore! You mother– … you don't have any brains! How can he take care of your herd, he made them stamp and ruin my entire field. Come here and look … orey! If it happens again, I'll tie him up and have him flogged! Look at him, look at that young son of a … look how he's crying …' he screamed.

Bandanaggadu saw the young one crying, laughed and said, 'Orey, stop this, you stupid wretch. Unable to drive the buffaloes, you are crying! You shameless rogue … go, drive them home.'

'I'm not able to control them.'

'How will they be controlled? You're caressing them – you must beat the hell out of them.'

'Dorasani asked me not to beat them.'

'Did the dorasanamma say that? As for the dorasani, she will say whatever pleases her! But ask her to tend the cattle one day without beating them, then she'll realise. The dorasani doesn't even know about the dora. How can she know about the cattle … come, come …' and said, 'Ay! … this way … this way … why has this become a blind herd! They seem to have forgotten the way home … may this herd be destroyed!' He ran behind the herd, and with the stick in his hand he started beating to death the ones that he could lay hands on.

When they were running helter-skelter, he ordered them, 'Get home. Otherwise I'll skin you alive today.

'Who the hell named you Sankurattirigadu! It would have been better to name you Sannasigadu, useless fellow. You stupid wretch,' he made fun of Sankurattirigadu all the way home.

By the time Sankurattirigadu went to the backyard all the buffaloes had appeared, each standing at its own post.

Then the young fellow thought …

'Maybe it's necessary to thrash cattle the way one has to thrash cattle.'

BHANUMATHI HAD THE reputation of being very beautiful in that village and in the neighbouring villages too. Like a sandalwood doll. Long hair. Her eyes and nose, as if they were sculpted. Slim waist. Good height. Whatever saree she wore, the saree attained beauty. If one were to describe her, it would be best to do so in the manner Puranam Sastrigaru spoke of the beauties in the Harikathas. While listening to the descriptions in the Harikathas, the women would smile and think, 'Perhaps that woman would look like our Bhanumathamma.'

This beauty is the person Yerra Suryam 'wedded'. Silk shirt, *Glasco* (Glasgow) pancha, the strong scent of perfume, rings, cigarette between fingers, paan in mouth – this was normally Yerra Suryam's get-up. He would always roam the streets of Gudivada Pati in this get-up.

If asked, 'Why do you keep going to Gudivada?' he would say, 'How long do you want me to sit at home? Just like that, I'll go to Raju Hotel, drink coffee and come.'

He also told a few truths. But he would not tell everything.

It was true that he would go and drink coffee at Raju Hotel. After that, he would buy a 'really good' paan in the paan shop next to it, get on a rickshaw and say, 'Get going!'

The rickshaw-pullers there were not in the habit of asking such people 'where to' or 'how much will you give'.

That fellow too would get going. He would go through lanes and bylanes and stop at a place. This one would get off, turn towards the rickshaw-puller, laugh sheepishly, and say, 'Wait here,' and go away.

He would come back from there to the waiting rickshaw, go and, get down at the centre of the town, roam about here and there for a while, ogle at the women walking on the road, if possible, walk a little distance with them, while away some time in this manner, engage another rickshaw and return to the village.

He would have a bath, heartily eat the dishes cooked by his wife who would have not eaten anything, and go to bed.

Though Bhanumathi was pained by her husband's behaviour at first, she soon delved into the puranas, thought of the stories of Savitri, Anasuya and Arundhati and their being termed *pativratas*[*], swallowed her tears and felt content.

---

[*] Refers to happily married women who considered the husband as god.

One evening, Sorajjem was covering the hens under the basket. The red-feathered hen got on to the top of the big basket, and jumped on to the cattle shed. Sorajjem who was chasing it saw a woman come out of the room where ploughs were kept. The dora came right behind her and began shouting at the palerus, 'Why haven't you milked the big-horned one as yet? What have you been doing all this while?'

Sorajjem felt her legs and hands tremble. She caught hold of the red-feathered hen, came to the backyard, covered it under the basket, and in two minds thought, 'Should I tell dorasanamma or not, should I tell dorasanamma or not?'

Finally, unable to contain herself, she went near the dorasanamma who was sitting in front of the stove, and said, 'Dorasani ... just a little while ago ... when I was covering the hens ... some woman came out of our plough room ...' and stood looking at the dorasanamma, anxious to know what she would do.

Bhanumathamma, as she stoked the wood in the fire, said, without looking up, 'Who was she?'

'I don't know ... I didn't know in that darkness. She's not someone known to me.'

'Did she fall from the sky? Is there anyone in the village you don't know? How did she look? Was she beautiful?'

'I don't know ... I didn't see properly. In the darkness she looked like a tumma stump. When dora does such things, why do you keep quiet?' Sorajjem asked angrily.

By then, tears had welled up in Bhanumathi's throat, 'What else can I do but keep quiet. I must hang myself. I'll do that too some time.'

'Chi! That's not what I mean, please. Scream at doragaru.'

'You're a young bitch. What will you understand?' Bhanumathi said, and sat right there and burst out crying.

Sorajjem's mind was disturbed.

'Mahalakshmamma would pour out all her anger on her husband. She would abuse him heartily to his face. This dorasanamma does not know anything else but to cry. Poor thing,' she thought. Sorajjem's anger against the dora increased all the more. Now when she saw Bhanumathi cry, Sorajjem felt sad and consoled the dorasanamma saying, 'Don't cry, ammagoru!' Bhanumathi felt like embracing Sorajjem.

'No one has your heart, Sorajjem,' she said and cried for a while longer.

EVEN BEFORE A month was up, Sorajjem had to stop working in Bhanumathigaru's house.

That day, all of a sudden, Bhanumathi left for Gudivada. Vanajakshi's son came and scared Bhanumathi saying that Vanajakshi had labour pains. Her relatives would always ask Bhanumathi to come and help out whenever in need. Added to it was the fact that Vanajakshi was Bhanumathi's maternal aunt's daughter.

Bhanumathi left the work she was doing in Sorajjem's hands, engaged a cart and took Vanajakshi to a hospital in Gudivada. Before she left, she instructed Sorajjem several times about things at home, 'Don't go home today. Get your mother and both of you sleep here. I don't know when the dora will come. If he comes, you can go. If he doesn't, don't leave the house and go. I'll also inform Naggadu. Grain baskets and such, odds and ends are all out in the open,' and went away.

When Naggadu left, after feeding the cattle in the night, the only people left in the Lanka-sized house were Sankurattirigadu and Sorajjem. After finishing all the chores, the two of them sat on the terrace steps facing the street, with their heart in their mouth.

When Sorajjem told Sankurattirigadu in the evening, 'Go, get my mother,' he said, 'We don't need anyone else. Can't we sleep by ourselves?' Both thought so and kept quiet. It was after six, and inside the compound in such a big house they felt as if they were in a jungle. The house was a little away from the village. Moreover … trees all around. During darker days, by six or seven it would feel as if one were in a jungle.

'I'm frightened,' said the young fellow.

'Stupid! Why fear?' Sorajjem bullied him. But she too was scared.

'The dora doesn't come back every day, no? How does the dorasani stay all alone in such a big house?'

'Don't know. Maybe she prays to Anjaneya.'

'So, let's too think of him.'

The two of them sat for a while without speaking.

When a cat jumped from the wall, Sankurattirigadu yelled loudly, 'Olammo!'

'Chi! Wretched Sannasi! Keep quiet!' scolded Sorajjem.

'I'll go get your mother.'

'I'll sit on the threshold facing the street. Go run and get her. You must come back as if you've not left.'

'I'll come back just now,' Sankurattirigadu said, and ran out. Sorajjem sat on the platform in the street.

She felt frightened to sit all alone even in the street. She took one jump from the platform to the entrance of the house, closed the doors facing the street, and stood trembling vigorously. The house that was bustling everyday looked woebegone without the dorasanamma.

When Sorajjem sat thinking, she heard a knock on the door, jumped up and opened the door, and shouted, 'Oh! You've come.'

As soon as the door was opened, the 'Mala one' was seen.

Sorajjem felt as if all her fear had been removed. She thought, 'Hamma! The dora has come. No need to fear anymore.'

Suryam saw an auspicious sign the moment he stepped into the house.

'Why haven't you gone yet?' he asked.

'No, dora. Dorasanamma has gone to Gudivada engaging a cart. Vanajakshammagaru was having a lot of labour pains. She took her to the hospital.'

'Are you alone?'

'Yes. Just now, Sankurattirigadu left to get my mother.'

'Will she come?'

'Why won't she come? There are two hens, isn't it? She'll cover them up, eat if there is any food and come. We thought you may not come and so we thought the three of us could sleep here.'

'What if I've come? All of you can still sleep here.'

'Why? You've come. I'll go home now.'

'You can go, but …' he said, took off his shirt, gave the shirt to her saying, 'Go, keep it inside.' Sorajjem took the shirt and went into the bedroom.

Yerra Suryam closed the doors facing the street and entered the bedroom.

As Sorajjem was about to leave the room, he said, 'Get me some water.'

On the way to the house, Suryam had gone to the fallow fields. He saw Chandri gathering the long strips fallen from the male palm. By then it had grown pitch dark. Suryam became courageous, went near her and asked, 'What are you doing?'

'Everyone knows this dora's character,' Chandri thought.

As Chandri was a bit old, she was not scared, and said, 'Can't you see?'

'Hey, hey, hey,' he laughed a sheepish laugh and was about to hold her hand.

She shook off his hand, and said contemptuously, 'What's this? It's enough. Now leave.'

'What? Why are you so arrogant? We are from the same village. Is there no concern for each other? Take ten rupees. Did I say I wouldn't give it to you?'

'Save your respect and go away from here. You say you'll give ten rupees, ten rupees! Ask your woman to earn that money,' said Chandri.

'You mother– …' and with another vulgar abuse, he was about to pounce on her.

Chandri swiftly took out the sickle from her basket. He hesitated.

'When I repeated your own words to you, your male ego is hurt. Did you think we weren't such people?' she said, swung the sickle and walked away briskly.

When he came back home disappointed, his excitement surfaced once again.

'Take the water,' Sorajjem was about to give him water in a steel glass.

Yerra Suryam took hold of Sorajjem's hand, put the glass down, laughed sheepishly, and pulled her on to the bed saying, 'Come here.'

It was then that Sorajjem understood the dora's intention.

'What's this … wait … this is not done,' she said, twisted and struggled and got rid of his hold.

'I'll give you ten rupees. Don't worry, I won't tell your dorasani.'

'Chi … Get up!' Sorajjem was about to run away angrily.

Again he caught hold of her hand tightly.

'I'll bite you … what do you think …' Sorajjem said, raining fire on him with her eyes.

Suryam was not afraid of sin.

Brute animal strength, caste strength and wealth strength were giving him encouragement.

Sorajjem's helpless state, youth and low caste … were encouraging him all the more.

'It's not wrong … I'll give you a lot of money.'

'Who needs your money, leave me,' Sorajjem said, pulled away and ran towards the cattle shed.

'Sorajjem! Open the door!' with this shout from Sankurattirigadu, Suryam turned into a corpse.

He let go off Sorajjem, went into the room and bolted the door.

Sorajjem opened the door to the street from the cattle shed and came out.

The next evening, Sankurattirigadu told Bhanumathamma the whole story.

Sorajjem did not step on that threshold again.

PADDALU FELT MISERABLE that she could not talk of the horrendous act that Yerra Suryam wanted to commit on her daughter.

Believing that it was her mistake to have sent her grown-up daughter to work, that it was her wretched fate to have sent her, she told Sorajjem and Sankurattirigadu not to tell anyone, and began taking Sorajjem along with her for coolie work she got now and then.

Sorajjem had been going for coolie work for the past six months.

Paddalu, Sorajjem, Bodi, Koti, Ratti and forty other women coolies went to plant the saplings in Pedda Ramaiahgaru's thirty-acre field, their sarees tucked in, each one got down and were going about the whole field.

Ramaiahgaru's third son, Sivaprasad – who was not able to study no matter how much he was pushed up – was bossing over them.

'Get down! Osi, you mother– ... You come much after dawn as if you are queens come to see the estates. After you come, you trample for hours as if you are ankle-belled horses! Half the money we pay for your coolie is sheer waste, you whores! Get down, get down.'

'Just because we keep quiet because you are the younger dora, you use the choicest abuses. Will you please hold your tongue?'

'What's it, you mother–? ... Are you asking me to shut up?'

'Why are using such harsh words?'

'Harsh words? Isn't it wrong for you to come late?'

'Were we late? We've come at the time we come daily.'

'We don't know how to see the clock. We go by the break of dawn.'

'That's enough. Start your work, you mother– ...'

Nagi added, 'Sinnabbayigoru! Why do you abuse like that? Get the work done properly. We've come to earn for doing coolie work, not for such abuses!'

As the arguments and counterarguments between the women coolies and the younger dora were going on, far away from beneath the palm tree along the bunds the pedda dora was seen walking slowly towards them.

'Okay, get going, get going, my father's coming. Get down quickly. Yenkatesiga, throw down the sticks,' the younger dora said, feeling very frightened.

All the anger that was burning in the coolies cooled down the moment they saw Pedda Ramaiahgaru. There was commotion and screams that even when after the pedda dora had arrived, no work had begun.

Yenkatesigadu was throwing the bundles of paddy saplings so the coolies could catch them.

On the whole, by the time Pedda Ramaiah came on to the bund, all the coolies were seriously involved in their work.

He came and yelled, 'What's this, Pesadu? I thought by now an acre would have been done. But on reaching I feel they have just got into the fields.'

'How could it be done? They have just come, after eating and belching.'

'Why do you lie like that? Without allowing us to get down into the fields, you started to have a quarrel with us.'

'What quarrel?' asked Pedda Ramaiah.

'What's there? He used the choicest abuses, naming each and every one of us.'

'Yera! May your mother's stomach burn! Is this how you get work done by those who have come?'

'I didn't say anything, nanna.'

'Orey! Don't open your mouth. Get the hell out of here and be at the place where the saplings are grown. Go ask them to pluck the saplings quickly and hand them over. Go, get going.'

Pedda Ramaiah always tried to see that his son was nowhere near the women coolies.

'*Oo, oo*. Finish it, finish it … Osey Paddalu! Who's next to you? She doesn't seem to know how to plant properly? Is that how you plant? Does she know that she has got into Pedda Ramaiah's fields? … plant them close, close to each other. Ask them to plant a couple at a time, a couple at a time, ask them to put it … who is that? Nagamma's daughter? Has she grown up so much? …'

'No, she's my daughter,' said Paddalu.

'Your daughter? Osey, may your stomach boil! She's grown up. I saw her a long time ago when Bemmamgaru hoisted the flag. Rajalakshmi or what's her name? Wasn't it he who named her?' Saying this, he stepped into the water and began levelling the field.

'It's Sorajjem.'

'Some Rajjem or the other … two at a time, two at a time. Osey, Nagi, why that bride's walk? Weed, weed … Come forward … come, come! It's getting late. This way, don't know how late it'll be when it's done.'

'What?'

'Complete your work till that big bund.'

'Up till that big bund? How many acres will that be?'

'How many are there, just eight.'

'What eight? It'll easily be eleven or twelve acres.'

'Why twelve? These are all the forty acres I have.'

'What are you saying? You've employed forty people … Even if you calculate at seven per acre, we cannot do even half, not more than six acres. But you are saying till the big bund. Even if you say it's less, it won't be a cent lesser than ten acres.' Saying this, each argued in her own manner.

Sorajjem felt like laughing at the pedda dora.

'These doras wish to give less coolie and get more work done,' Sorajjem thought, as if she had learnt a new thing.

ONE EVENING, SORAJJEM who was gathering cow dung was surprised to see Sayitrakka slip by like a thief next to Pesadugaru's hay stack, and stand at a distance. After a little while, Pesadugaru too came out with a cigarette in his mouth and went over the fields to the other side and climbed on to the bund.

Sayitrakka was gasping with fear, walking quickly and was about to cross Sorajjem.

'Why are you coming from there, Sayitrakka?'

'From where?'

'Chi! Why this wretched life ... Mother of four, aren't you ashamed?'

Sayitrakka did not deny. She hung her head.

'What else can I do?'

'Jump into the canal and die.'

'Then, you look after my kids ... I'll die ... did you think this was enjoyable for me?' she said. Showing the ladies fingers in the basket, she continued, 'Here, he gave these. He also gave a rupee. How do you think the children's bellies are filled every meal time? Did you think your drunkard of a brother-in-law worked hard and supported us? If I didn't have any responsibilities like you, I too would say things.'

'Even so?'

'Tell what other way there is. Mother and children, all of us must drown in the canal. That wretched useless fellow has been bothering me for a week, and without listening to me dragged me there. Will the big people let a Mala bitch alone when they see her? ... You're young. Be careful. What's of my life? I've already been spoilt,' her voice became hoarse and she started crying.

After that, Sorajjem saw many Sitas, Damayantis and Ahalyas like that in fields, streams, haystacks, dirt heaps and on the threshing floor.

All of them would appear shrivelled in shame.

They would be happy that they got a little bit of paddy or vegetables or yam or cobs or green gram or black gram and go home carrying them in baskets in their arm pits.

If one were to find the doings of rich, respectable people, one could find them in the baskets of these women.

AT ONCE THERE was news in the entire Malapalli. Bemmamgaru appeared to have bought a *tactor.* That would of itself dig and plough. It would harvest. It would also haul paddy and such, and grass and such. Did you know the secret, there was no need to yoke bullocks to it!

'Bemmamgaru seems to have bought an engine pump too. With that one can draw water too. Even for the other doras, he would charge something per hour and have water drawn for them too!' You bet, the Mala and Madiga pallis were heated up with this news.

On the one hand, the clearing of fields was drawing to a close. Watering the fields, ploughing, levelling, furrowing – all the coolies were worried that all these jobs were gone.

Four years ago, when they asked for a hike in the coolie rates and that horrible incident took place, all of them put paid at one place.

When they thought that they should ask for a hike this year, in the meanwhile, this bad news.

Coolies and such, and children and such – all of them gathered around Bemmamgaru's *tactor*, saw it and returned. After they saw it, they were less scared. New news went around that it could not do everything in the village, and that they would need coolies like before.

'This time, no matter what, we must ask them to raise the coolie rates,' Shamelu placed this before a number of people.

'Orey, enough of bravery! Asking for a hike ... we'll ask for a hike! Isn't it only because we asked for a hike that our people met such a fate? Don't ask again in your lifetime. If they think of it, they will raise it themselves. If not, let's consider it our fate and do the work. Let's not ask for a raise or a cut,' said one scared person.

'Keep quiet, you brainless fellow! Fearing death, will we see to it that we don't have food? If they say they would pay the same coolie rate today that they did during our grandfathers' days, who will work? If we have to die, we'll die, but how many days can we keep our mouths shut?' Shamelu said in disgust.

After a lot of discussion, they decided to approach Bemmamgaru.

'Bemmamgoru is a bit of a good man. At least once in four or five years, he finds out the condition of Malapalli. Let's go and ask him. He will raise the rate.'

Men and women all agreed to this.

They went to Bemmamgaru's house.

That house was not the old house. He had demolished it and built a two-storeyed house. After Independence, having joined 'Congirechu'*, he easily climbed up the ladder. Now he owned one-third of the land in that village.

As the coolies had thought, he would come to Malapalli once in four or five years, hold his nose and sneeze out the few words in his nose ...

why all of them ought to vote for 'Congiresu',

what Gandhigaru said,

how even though Dharmaraja had lost because of some deception, how dharma finally won and he became king,

Harischandra's adherence to truth,

Krishna's preaching the Gita,

Sitamma's hardships,

... he would say all this and keep asking them to vote only for 'Congiresu'.

Though all the coolies came to the same conclusion that there was nothing Bemmamgaru did not know, Bemmamgaru would meet them every four or five years and have it reconfirmed by them.

When all of them now gathered in front of Bemmamgaru's bungalow, Brahmam came out ...

* There is a pun on 'race' that allows people to quickly climb up the ladder.

'What's it? How come all of you have come together?' he asked, enquiring their well-being.

'What's it, Paddalu? How's your daughter?' he asked noticing Paddalu in the crowd.

When Bemmamgaru remembered and asked about her daughter, Paddalu almost fainted.

'Here she is. Have a look at her,' Paddalu said, overwhelmed.

Brahmamgaru almost fainted on seeing Sorajjem.

'Osey, you … is this her? I don't know why I couldn't recognise our Sorajjem. How much she has grown! … *aa* … has grown like a horse.'

'Where has she grown? Beady legs, beady hands. She doesn't have even a stomachfull of food – your Sorajjem,' Paddalu said, intending to make Brahmamgaru's heart melt.

'Why doesn't she have food? What do you lack? You work hard. You eat a stomachfull and sleep well. You are able to digest stones … Sorajjem, come here! Come here!' As Brahmam called her, Sorrajem was a bit scared and shy.

'Go,' four or five scolded Sorajjem.

Sorajjem went four steps closer and stood. On her checked *parikini*[*], she had mandaram-coloured[†] paita. A tamarind-flowered blouse. Hair plaited tight, eyes large, back that was slim and curved at the waist – Brahmam noticed this, was excited, placed his hand on the girl's waist and said, 'How grown up you are, Sorajjem!' caressed her entire back, caressed her shoulders, and as his excitement had not abated, was about to put his hands on her back again, Sorajjem moved back to a distance as if she felt shy. As Sorajjem's body was not used to deception, it revolted against Brahmamgaru's caresses.

She felt inwardly more disgusted than she felt when a centipede had fallen from a grass heap and brushed against her back a few days ago.

After talking to Sorajjem, the actual matter came up.

The coolies asked for a hike in coolie rates.

'Osey! That's all, is it? Fine,' said Brahmamgaru.

---

[*] A full-length skirt.

[†] Red-coloured

Everyone was shocked, wondering how the task had been accomplished so fast!

These people did not say that it should be hiked by this much.

He too did not say he would have it increased by that much.

'Okay, I'll look into it,' said Brahmamgaru.

The coolies applauded and turned back.

'Come and see me now and again, Sorajjem,' Brahmamgaru ogled at her, and let go, unable to let go.

A thunderbolt of a news – before a week was over, Brahmamgaru's tractor brought coolies from the Nizam and dumped them in the village.

The coolies of the village were shocked.

It seemed it would go again and bring another tractorful.

In the cattle sheds of Brahmamgaru and Rajendra Prasadgaru, the coolies from the Nizam were roasting dried fish in a hurry.

The whole village was filled with smell of dried fish.

Wrapping big, big head cloths, without proper clothing on their bodies, the Nizam's coolies were going about innocently in the bazaars.

Once again all the coolies went to Brahmamgaru's house, this time bristling with anger and fury.

'How can you starve the coolies in the village and feed the coolies from the Nizam?' each one asked in their distinct ways – angrily, a little less angrily, or even a bit less angrily.

Brahmam said calmly, 'Arey! Don't create a problem. You said the coolie was not enough. You said that it had to be increased. That meant you wouldn't work if it wasn't hiked, right? The doras don't have the wherewithal to increase. Only if we are able to increase … we ought to ask you to come and work. Otherwise, we have to fend for ourselves, isn't it? Isn't that so? Why should we quarrel unnecessarily? … I'm not Purushottamarao, to kill one or two of you, call others giving the same coolie and cause a rift within you … As for violence, I dislike it very much. Man must not exploit another man … I haven't beaten or abused any one of you … I haven't tied up your hands! I haven't shackled your feet! Hold your stomachs and go wherever you get higher wages. Who can say no?

Poor things, you have to look out for your livelihoods … What else can you do? What else can I do?'

Realising that the anger of a poor man harmed his own lips, they turned around boiling with rage, not knowing what else to do.

HALF THE PEOPLE in Malapalli had no work. The Nizam's coolies had come in three batches. There were also small fights between them and the village coolies in the bazaar.

They had to forget their getting coolie work in the village. Those who were able to find work reconciled themselves to the wages they received.

The doras smiled to themselves that the 'disease of the coolies was curbed' in the village. Why just disease, their lives were curbed too. With hunger, with infectious diseases, the old and decrepit, with dead children, with broken-down houses, entire Malapalli had collapsed. All the coolies who had stood together till then were strewn around because of failing determination.

Paddalu's house was among the twenty or thirty houses that had lost its livelihood. Though Sorajjem would roam around trees and pit holes and bring snails and wild roots, even if she dug and brought kale roots, it had become a Herculean task for them to tide over one meal.

Rami and Nagi went away to Guduru, thinking they would find coolie work in the graphite mines there.

Some men were going to Gudivada and Bezavada, hoping to earn a living driving rickshaws.

'I believe it isn't so bad as here in the Nellore area …' Sayitri said to Paddalu one day.

'Even death doesn't come to me. If I die, the girl will manage to live somehow,' said Paddalu crying.

'That's enough. Keep quiet. If you die, I'll jump into the east lake and I will die too,' said Sorajjem.

'Keep quiet! What do we achieve by dying? Don't we have to live till we have life?' screamed Sayitri.

'What life now! Wretched life! I don't have the energy to step out of the hut. Wherever I want to go …' Paddalu broke down.

Sayitri chatted for a while and left, but in the afternoon she came screaming, 'Osey, Paddakka! Paddakka ... A Nellore man has come. I believe he needs forty to fifty workers. Come, let's go. I'll let Lachi and Yenki know,' she ran even as the words had not left her mouth.

'Tie up your things,' she screamed from a distance and disappeared.

'What should we tie up?' Paddalu said, and slumped as she was unable to think of anything. It was Sorajjem who took it upon herself to put a few clothes and tie them in an old saree, and put a few vessels in a basket.

The hen and the dog were finished a long while ago. By the time the two bundles were done, there was nothing left in the hut. They arranged the old sunken sling cot and two cracked pots in a corner, covered them with a mat, and tied a string to the thatch at the threshold.

They picked up a bundle each.

Lachi and Yenki came that way with a small bundle each.

When Sayitri came and disappeared in a jiffy, they stood in front of Paddalu's hut and shouted, 'Osey, Sayitri, Sayitri'.

Those dirty lanes were agog with the screams of coolies.

On each one's head, a gunny sack or a big plate. At their feet, two or three kids.

'We're going out of the village,' the kids were thrilled.

The young and the old were hanging like strips of bark. No one knew how far they had to walk or where they had to reach. When some 'big man' came, they followed him. They did not bargain what the coolie rates would be, or anything else.

'Get going,' each one was abusing the other.

Some could not drag their feet.

They would go back into their huts.

As if there were some precious stones or gems there. They would look at those cracked pots again, come out and tie up the thatch doors.

Paddalu crept into her hut twice and came out.

After an hour the coolie mob moved, dragging its feet.

How difficult it was for them to leave those dirty lanes, only those who were born and raised there would know!

A village they lived in since birth.

Fifty-year-old people were also in the group. Taking a step forward, Yenki turned towards the village and prostrated once again saying, ‘Don’t know when we’ll be back.’

Four or five others did the same.

‘Where will we come back!’ said someone.

‘Don’t say that, amma,’ said Paddalu.

Sorajjem kept turning time and again for a last look.

Sorajjem, now sixteen, left home empty bellied, seeking a livelihood in places far away.